SEAL SECURITY BOOK 4
LUCA

**AUTHOR
SUSIE MCIVER**

UNTITLED

I dedicate this book to my wonderful husband Larry, who puts up with me writing at all different times of the day and night.

MORE BOOKS BY SUSIE MCIVER

SEAL SECURITY
My Book
FBI SPECIAL AGENTS
My Book
BAND OF NAVY SEALS
My Book
ARMY RANGERS SPECIAL OPS
My Book

Copyright © 2023 by Susie McIver

All rights reserved.

No part of this publication may be reproduced, distributed, or transmitted in

any form or by any means, including photocopying, recording, or other electronic or mechanical methods, without the prior written permission of

the publisher, except as permitted by U.S. copyright law. For permission request, contact Susie McIver susie.mciver@yahoo.com

Book Cover by Amanda Walker

❀ Created with Vellum

1

LUCA

I thought my eyes were seeing things when she came running down the hill out of control with Ethan's wife, Sara. The one woman I never forgot or thought to see again was running straight for me, ready to plow into all of us. Here I was in Italy, and here she was. It was like fate for me to find her again—if you believe in that kind of stuff. I don't.

I knew when she saw me, she recognized me. She turned around and tried a different route. All that did was make her run backward until she skidded down the hill. I followed her and picked her up. She looked at me, and I grinned, then kissed her on her mouth.

"Please put me down! Where did you come from? Why are you here? You are not allowed to kiss me."

"So, you must be Cassie, Sara's sister. How come you never shared that beautiful name with me?" I started patting her hair, removing pebbles and debris from her long braid.

"I am. What is your name? I don't remember you sharing your name with me. We weren't into names those two days."

"Luca Thatcher. It's nice meeting you, Cassie."

"Stop patting my head, for Christ's sake. Please put me down. Ethan," she yelled, "tell your friend to put me down!"

I chuckled. Damn, she still smelled the same—of oranges and vanilla. I could feel myself getting hard and was glad I was wearing my fatigues. I will never forget my two days with her. How could I? It was engraved into my mind. I stayed hard the entire time we were together. We barely slept; if I wasn't waking her, she was waking me up.

"Hush up," I said, looking into those beautiful eyes. "Your knees and hands are all scraped up. Are you in pain?"

"No, I'm not... Maybe a little." *Are my eyes getting moist? Damn you, Cassie, do not allow a drop of water to leave your eyes.* "Please don't tell my sister about that night."

"You mean two nights."

"Whatever, just don't tell her."

I carried her into her grandfather's house and sat her down. She walked off and disappeared down a dark hallway. She was more beautiful than I remembered. She smelled so damn good; I could have nibbled on her neck. I remember those were the best two days of my life. Her skin was so soft. There was no spot on her beautiful body that I hadn't tasted.

Of course, I had only been out of prison for a few months when I met this beautiful woman with long blonde hair and emerald green eyes. I was in Ireland when I saw her sitting at the bar. She looked scared to death. I walked over and asked her why she was sitting alone.

"Because I wanted to see what it feels like to sit in a pub alone. I'm in Ireland, so I want to try new things. And what are you doing here?"

"I just finished a job here and am staying another week to check out this country. How about we leave this place and go to dinner?" We did just that then we went dancing. We ended up in the little cottage I had rented and had two magical nights together.

When she left, I tried to find her, but I had no luck. Now, here I was, and she'd just run straight into my arms. I couldn't believe my luck until I learned she was Ethan's sister-in-law. The things we did in that cottage. I have never enjoyed sex more than I did with Cassie.

I could have fallen hard for her if we had been together longer, so it *was good* that she left while I was in the shower. I left right after her that day and hadn't seen her since.

~

I LOOKED OVER AT ETHAN, who was still talking. "What the hell are you talking about?"

"Sara is scared because Cassie hasn't called her in over a week. She always calls every day. She's afraid this new guy Cassie met has something to do with her not calling."

"Which new guy did she meet? I thought she was living here in Oregon somewhere."

"She was, but she met someone when she returned to Italy to visit her family. She was supposed to come home this week. Sara doesn't want to upset her family because she's afraid her grandfather will go in with guns blazing. She did call and ask if they'd heard from Cassie. Her grandfather has been gone, and their parents are on a honeymoon. I would go, but the baby will be here any day now."

"So, I guess you want me to go looking for her? Where in Italy is she?"

"It has to be somewhere near where the family lives. She met the guy in town somewhere. Maybe you can ask around and see if someone has seen a beautiful woman with long blonde hair and green eyes."

"You do know I'm on vacation."

"Yes, that's why I'm asking you. Everyone else is busy. No one can find a missing person like you can."

"You should have told me a week ago if she hasn't called in a week. Okay, I'll call the airport."

"I've already done that. You can pick up your ticket when you get there. The plane leaves in two hours."

"What if I had said no?"

"I knew you wouldn't because you have sisters and a kind heart."

"Oh, please never say I have a kind heart out loud again. The team would never let me live that down. I'm the bad guy from prison."

Ethan laughed. "Thank you, Luca."

"Hey, you're my teammate, making you my brother. Of course, I will find your sister-in-law. If she shows up, call me."

"I will. Thanks."

2

CASSIE

I felt an uneasy feeling wash over me when George said he had to go by his house and get his wallet before taking me to see some beautiful botanical gardens. He said he wanted to share the beauty of the gardens with me. I knew something was off; I didn't feel right.

I knew he lived way out of town. He got out of his car and walked over to my side. "I'm just going to stay in the car while you grab your wallet."

"No, you're coming in with me."

"I don't want to go in with you. I'll wait right here." He grabbed my arm and started pulling. "Let go of my arm," I cried. You're hurting me. What are you doing?"

"Okay, I'll let go of your arm." He let go of my arm but started pulling me by my hair. I was fighting and kicking him. I knew I couldn't let him pull me into his house. I was trying to bite his hand. I tried everything to get away from this crazy bastard. I knew if I didn't get away, he would kill me.

I fought him as much as I could. I kicked and pulled him anywhere I could reach. I knew he would rape me and then kill me. He slugged me in the face, and I blacked out. When I opened my eyes, he sat in a chair, staring at me.

"Get your ass up. I'm hungry. You get to cook me dinner tonight."

"What are you doing? This is crazy. You can't do this. It's against the law. My family will kill you for doing this."

"Oh honey, you haven't seen crazy yet. You'll get in there and cook my steak unless you want me to beat your ass."

I tried running to the door, but he laughed before jumping up. He grabbed me, slugged me, and I fell and hurt my side. I looked around, and two naked women were lying on the floor. Tears rolled down their faces. I looked at that man who I thought was kind and loving only hours ago, and all I could see was this monster. "Who are you?"

"I'm someone you're going to wish you never met. Isn't that right, ladies? We'll see if she's stronger than the other ones were. Now, get in there and cook my dinner."

I picked myself up. "Show me where the kitchen is." *Maybe I can find a knife and kill him. Or perhaps, I can hit him in the head with something.*

"Start walking." When we got to the doorway of the kitchen, I stopped. The place was filthy but that was the least of my worries. He kicked me hard with his foot against my back. I flew across the room. I hit my head on the wall, and it knocked me out. When I woke up again, he was naked. That scared the hell out of me—more than I was scared already. *I have to get away from this crazy man.*

I cooked his steak and sat with the other young ladies on the floor. "You're not allowed to talk to anyone. No matter what, you're not allowed to talk to anyone. If you don't follow my rules, I'll kill you."

"Aren't you going to kill me anyway?"

"Not good to be a mouthy bitch either. Just ask the

ladies?" I looked over, and the women were shaking their heads. "Did I tell you I don't like smart-asses? So, if you talk smart back to me, you get a kick. I will kick you whenever you open your mouth and say something I don't like."

I looked out the window, and it was already dark outside. *How am I going to get away from this man? He's crazy. He must be a serial killer.* My mind was going wild, thinking about what he was, how many people he's killed. *I have to get away to get help for these other women. It looks like I'm the strongest one between us three.*

"Drink this." He had a glass of red stuff. It looked like Kool-Aid; that reminded me of Jim Jones, the man who made all of his cult followers drink that fucking Kool-Aid and killed them.

"I'm not thirsty."

"It doesn't matter if you're thirsty or not. Drink it, or I will cut her head off," he said, pointing a knife to a woman sitting on the floor beside me.

The woman shook her head at me. She didn't want me to drink it, but I knew he would cut her head off in front of us, so I drank it. Nothing happened. About ten minutes later, I could feel myself slipping away. He drugged me just like I knew he would.

When I came to again, I kicked my leg out and felt my feet hit the wall instantly. I tried to move but it was cramped. There was someone next to me. I didn't have a stitch of clothes on. I decided against screaming. I took a deep breath to steel myself. I heard something. "Who's here? Who is that?" I pushed my arm to see if I could touch someone, hoping that it wasn't him. What if he was going to rape me? That would be the only reason why I was naked. I touched someone but it wasn't him. It was a girl and she wasn't moving much. I touched her neck to feel a pulse. I could feel one, but it was so slow it was barely there. She flinched against my touch.

"Be careful. I'm on the other side," a soft voice said.

I raised my head and turned it in the direction of her voice. "Who are you?"

"Jana, and that's Kathy on the other side. She's not doing too good. We went to school together," she whispered so low I could barely hear her. "Kathy's been here longer than I have. There are other women here too. They're in the other rooms. He takes turns raping us. Some women have already died. He ensures we are so drugged up that we can't walk, fight back, or ever leave here.

"He doesn't allow us to have water. That's also why there are so many dirty dishes. He won't let us do the dishes because he says we'll take a drink of water. Only the newer ladies cook. The ones who have been here longer can't stand because he keeps us drugged up."

"We have to find a way out of here."

"Be careful," Jana shushed me. I spoke too loudly. "If he hears us talking, he'll kick us until we black out. Let's not talk anymore."

I could tell she was scared. "Okay, we won't talk." I lay there for a while and heard the door open, and the closet door unlocked. I hurried up and pulled myself in front of Kathy. I didn't imagine I could climb over her so fast. I wasn't strong, I even felt a bit woozy still, but they'd been in this situation for much longer than I had. I couldn't imagine Kathy going through more, given the state she was in.

He laughed when he saw me. I didn't know what to expect. "I want my clothes. You have no right taking them," I snarled.

"I see you haven't learned anything yet. Get the hell out

LUCA

of my way." He grabbed my hair, pulled me up and out of the closet, and pulled Jana out next. He made me sit and watch as he raped her. I couldn't move my limbs. It was as though every bit of strength that I had a moment ago had disappeared. I couldn't bear to watch him rape that poor woman.

I could cry, and that's what I did. I closed my eyes and refused to watch him hurt her. I cried silent tears that ran down my face.

It was the third day now, at least; that's what I thought it was. I was confused because there was black paint on the windows and I couldn't tell any difference in time. I knew we were in the basement. Jana told me he kept us down there in case someone came by.

All of a sudden, he came in there shouting at me about another woman who died. "This is your fault! I will rape you now since I can't rape her!"

"You fucker, you killed her. She didn't die, you killed her. She was murdered. I would show you I could kick your ass if I weren't so drugged up. You are a piece of shit and will pay for everything you have done. My family will come after you, and you will die. You fucker!"

He started laughing. I knew Kathy was who he was talking about. I noticed Jana was getting weaker too. Pretty soon, it would be her falling asleep and not waking up. He slapped me across the face.

I lay there like a dead person, as he raped me. Jana said he wanted us to scream and fight because it excited him. Screw that. I wasn't going to let him get excited.

I'd only had sex with two men. There was a guy in college and then Luca. The college guy knew as much about sex as I did, which was nothing. Luca knew everything about sex. This fucker's little weenie wasn't even hard. I wasn't worried he would rape me. He couldn't get it hard enough.

I should never have smirked. He jumped off me and started to hit me. I blacked out, and Jana told me later that he continued beating me for a while after I blacked out. I was planning to get him good... Or did I dream that? I'd had so many scary dreams in this place. I wondered if it was the red Kool-Aid

I was sitting in the corner of the room when I thought I heard glass breaking. The asshole must have thrown something. It felt like I'd been here for months. I was pretty much out of it with all the Kool-Aid I'd drank. Ever since he tried raping me, he had kept me tied up like he was afraid I would jump up and kill him. I would if I could. I listened to see if I could hear anything else. I knew I heard glass breaking.

The killer entered the room and stood behind the door, waiting for someone. I sat there with my eyes half closed. I was still in pain from the last beating. I didn't want another fist in my face.

The door opened further and I saw him. I couldn't believe my eyes. My Knight in Shining Armor had come to rescue me—Luca Thatcher. He shined his light on me. The door slammed into the killer's face. I refused to call him anything else. When Luca entered the room, his arm came out, and he shot that mother fucker.

Then I passed out for no damn reason at all. I guess my heart was so happy to see him that I fainted from shock.

3

LUCA

I had been in Italy for two days when I called Sara. "Could you send me a photo of Cassie and her boyfriend?"

"He isn't her boyfriend. She just said she met a guy. She hadn't even gone out with him yet, and then she called me and said he seemed nice. I don't know anything else. She snuck a photo of him for me; he doesn't like having his picture taken. So, she took it when he wasn't looking."

"Why did she take his photo?"

"Cassie watches real crime stories all the time. She doesn't trust anyone. She is always being careful except with you. I don't know what came over her when she was with you in Ireland for those two days. You must have really sweet-talked her into going with you. She usually sends me all kinds of information if she is on a date. But then again, she doesn't date too often. She didn't even tell me about you."

"Cassie and I laugh because she spends so much time with me on her phone instead of paying attention to her date, and again, except with you. That's why I know she's in trouble. I'll send you those pictures of the guy, and please call me as soon as you find her."

"I will. Try not to worry. Think of the baby."

"I'll try. Thank you, Luca, for giving up your vacation time."

"Don't worry about it. If Cassie is still in Italy, I'll find her."

I walked around the town square, knowing I would see more people. I didn't have any luck that day. It was late at night. I sat at the bar. When people came inside, I would show them the photo.

I had my phone face up when two ladies sat beside me. One of them blurted out, "That guy is creepy?"

I turned to her. "You know this guy?" I said.

"Not personally. He moved here maybe a year ago, and the ladies know to stay away from him. He usually hangs out around here at night. There was this woman who went out to dinner with him. She said he raped her. She didn't turn it in until a month later. The police said it would be her word against his. So, she dropped it. She had some of her friends take care of him instead."

"I need to find him. My friend was last seen with him, and it's been almost two weeks."

"You should talk to Catrina. She said he took her to his house."

"Where can I find her?"

"I'll call her and see if she'll talk to you. Hang on."

I watched her call, and then she was talking to whoever this Catrina was. She looked at me, "Catrina is on her way here. She's going to take you there herself."

"Great, how far away does she live from here?

"Here she is," she said, looking past me. "Catrina works here."

"Let me see the photo," Catrina said, reaching for my phone. "That's him, the scum bastard. I almost went to his house again to kill him. I took a gun with me. I wanted to shoot the fucker so he couldn't hurt anyone else. I wish I had killed him. I hope the bastard doesn't have your friend because he's a sick son of a bitch. I hope you have a gun with you. This guy carries one on him."

"Are you going to show me where he lives?"

"Yes, I'm showing you. I'm going to help you find your friend."

"I'll follow you. Then you can come back here. I'll take care of him myself, so you aren't involved. If he has Cassie, I'm going to kill him. Let's go."

He lived out of town. I followed Catrina for thirty minutes before she slowed down. She blinked her lights. I looked at the dark house, and the chills ran over me. I drove on, then I parked. She stopped and got out of her vehicle.

"When he brought me here for dinner, he took me to a room in the basement. I bet he has her there. I carried Mace with me, so I got away. I was damn lucky. Kill him."

"I will. You can leave. I don't want you involved." She nodded and walked back to her car. I had my gun out as I went to the house. It was so dark inside I couldn't see anything. If only the clouds would let the moon shine through. I went to the back of the house, where most basements had a door entry or windows.

This house was different. It had no doors, not even a back door. I went around the side, and there was a window at the bottom of the house. It had to be a basement window. What else would be that low to the ground? I tried to listen for something, but I heard nothing. All of the windows had black paint on them.

I couldn't get it opened. It was locked tight. I pulled my

sleeve down over my hand and broke the window. I didn't hear anything. I reached my hand inside to unlock it. Then I quietly lowered myself inside. It was dark. I couldn't see anything. I thought I heard something. I stood against the wall and listened.

What the heck is that noise? It's so strange. It's like a pitter-patter noise, like rats running in the attic. I wonder if he raises rats down here. Maybe he has a big snake he feeds them to. I felt my way across the room, staying close to the wall. I knew Cassie was here I could feel it in my bones. There was a door and I wasn't sure if I should open it.

I had my gun ready as I slowly turned the handle. I used my phone flashlight to look around. The room was empty. I saw two more rooms, and both doors were closed.

I pushed open the second door and saw nobody but heard someone. As I walked over and opened the closet door, I had a creepy feeling. A woman lay there naked, tied up, and beaten. I reached down and felt her neck to see if she was alive. I could barely feel a pulse, but she was breathing. I kept looking. *This guy is fucking crazy. How many women are here? Oh my God, what if he's killed Cassie?*

I went back to the first room and opened that closet. Two women were in there also. I didn't even have to feel for a pulse; I knew they were dead. I called the police, and then I went to the third room. I prayed Cassie would be in this room alive.

I opened the door; she was sitting on the floor. Her eyes looked at me and went to the left. I knew he was hiding behind the door. I grabbed hold of the door handle and slammed the door in his face. I heard him yell, and I stepped around the door and shot him. I wasn't going to take any chance that he'd get free.

I took the tape off Cassie's mouth, cut the ropes off her

hands and feet, and then slipped my jacket around her. She didn't have anything on. "Cassie, sweetheart, will you be okay while I check the house for more women?"

"Look in the closet. Hurry."

I opened the closet door, and two women were there. One of them looked up at me. The other one looked like she wasn't doing so well. I helped the one who could to walk over to where Cassie was, and the other one, I picked up and carried out after. I started rubbing Cassie's hands and feet where she was tied up. She didn't look that great.

"How are you doing?"

"He made us drink Kool-Aid. It had poison in it. Our legs and arms are so weak we can't stand alone. If I could get up, I would kill him again."

"He's dead. He'll never hurt anyone else."

"Oh my God, he's worse than I could imagine," Catrina said, standing in the doorway.

"Cassie, this is Catrina. She showed me where he lived." I saw Cassie dip her head like she was embarrassed. I looked at Catrina. "It's good for you that I was the first to shoot. Or you would have been another one of these women."

"I thought you might need help. How many women are here?"

I looked at Cassie. "Are there any more women here?"

Tears were rolling down Cassie's face. "That bastard took three of them somewhere yesterday. I don't know where. I don't even know if they were still alive. He wouldn't let me check the women. I hate even thinking this, but I'm afraid they were all dead. I think there might be some other dead women here. We need water. We have to wash the poison out of our system."

I ran and got some bottled water. When I returned, Cassie was helping the other women. They were all crying.

She took a sip of water and then passed it around to the women. I ran and checked the rest of the house.

"Luca, Luca, where are you?" I could hear the panic in her voice.

"I'm right here, sweetheart. I was checking the rest of the house. Where is Catrina?"

"She said she was going to check the garage."

I was trying to help another woman take a drink when I heard the police outside. I ran up the stairs and yelled for them, and they all came running down. There were four police who each had their guns drawn. "He's dead. I killed him. Is the ambulance coming?"

"They are already here. Oh fuck, how many women are here? These are the missing women. Are there more?"

I told the police about the two dead women in the other room. Cassie was talking to another one, telling him he had taken some women off yesterday. "I don't know how many women he has killed. He was crazy. I'm so glad he's dead. If I had a gun, I would have killed him myself."

I removed my shirt and put it over the woman staring at me as if I would attack her. She could be in shock. I slid my shirt over her head, and she finished putting it on.

"Cassie, I'm going to call Sara and let her know I found you." Cassie nodded. I walked away a little bit and called Ethan. I told him everything that was going on. I told him I would stay with Cassie as long as she needed me.

Ethan was in shock. He couldn't believe Cassie went through all of this fucking shit. "I'm going to call Cassie's parents," Ethan said, "they'll meet you at the hospital. I'm glad you killed him. People like that don't deserve a court case. I'll talk to Sara and explain what is happening, but I won't tell her the whole story. You can go back to Cassie now."

I walked back to Cassie, picked her up, and held her in my arms. She leaned against my chest. I looked down, and she was sleeping. She must have been afraid to sleep normally, afraid this bastard would kill her. But he kept them drugged so he could do whatever he wanted to her while she was out from the drugs.

I looked around, and Catrina was helping the other ladies. The EMTs were loading women in the ambulance.

My body shook. I was so angry. I followed the ambulance to the hospital. I walked in with them. There was no way in hell I was leaving Cassie's side. I didn't give a damn how mad they got or how much they yelled at me. I refused to budge.

"I want him to stay with me."

"Let him stay with her if that's what she wants," the doctor said, walking into the cubical.

"How are the other ones doing?"

"The other doctors are in there with them right now. They said they would have died if it wasn't for you. You are very brave."

"No, I wasn't brave. I was scared the entire time I was there. I'm a nurse, and there was nothing I could do because I couldn't walk and barely move my arms. I don't know what kind of poison he gave us."

"Cassie, where are you? I want to see my daughter right now," Dante demanded. He sounded like he was ready to kill everyone. I stepped out from behind the curtain, and Cassie's parents, Dante and Serena, hurried to where I was.

"Honey, we thought you had gone back to America. Please forgive me for not paying enough attention to know my daughter was missing. We love you so much."

I could tell Cassie was spacing out. Her mom looked at her. "Honey, look at me."

I walked closer and touched her. She jumped. She looked at her mom. "I want to shower."

"We might have to wait, sweetie."

"I don't want to wait. I have to take one now." I walked over to a doctor and asked where the showers were.

"We don't want the ladies to shower until we examine them."

"I don't give a fuck what you want. Cassie needs one now. She says she hasn't been raped. She has to wash all of this away now."

"It's down that hallway."

I went back to Cassie. "Come on, sweetheart. I'll help you." I picked her up, blanket and all. I started walking down the hall to the shower. Her parents were following us.

"Mom, please get me some clean clothes from Grandpa's."

"We'll go right now, honey. Are you sure you don't want me to help you shower?"

"Mom, Luca and I know each other. We met a couple of years ago..." She trailed off, not knowing what to say.

"We'll be here when you get back with the clothes," I said, walking away. Then I stopped again. "I'll take good care of Cassie, I promise." Her mom nodded and wiped tears off her face.

Cassie sniffed, trying to keep her tears away. I took the blanket off, stripped, and left my boxers on. I walked into the shower with her. I saw a bottle of shampoo and grabbed it. I gently washed her hair. Then I soaped her body. I felt her wrap her arms around me so that she could stand on her own.

The tears started to fall, and she couldn't stop sobbing. I held her close. She cried, "I couldn't save myself or those poor young women who died because that bastard killed them," she cried. "I don't know self-defense." I stood there with my arms wrapped around her. "You're strong, your chest is broad, and your muscles bulge. No one would dare try to kidnap you. You can take care of yourself."

She looked up at me, "I need to learn self-defense."

"Okay."

"Can you teach me how to kill someone who tries to kidnap me?"

"Yes. I can teach you that."

"Thank you."

"You're welcome." I turned and grabbed a towel, and dried her off. There were two gowns, so I put one on her and dried myself off. I took my boxers off and tossed them in the garbage.

I dressed and carried Cassie back to where we were. We heard him talking before we saw him. Cassie's grandfather was spitting mad. When he got to where we were, he stopped. He looked at Cassie, and then he looked at me. "I hope you killed that motherfucker."

"I did." He walked to Cassie and wrapped her in his arms.

"I'm sorry this happened to you, sweetheart. What can I do?"

"There isn't anything to do, Grandpa. Luca killed him. And he's going to teach me self-defense."

"Thank God Sara sent you here," he said, looking at me. "Her instinct was right." He looked back at Cassie, "Are they getting a room for you?"

"Grandpa, I don't want to stay here. I want to go home with you. Luca's going with us." Then she looked at me, "Are you staying with me until I get well and strong?"

"I will stay with you until you chase me off."

"I will never do that."

It wasn't long after that that her parents came back and gave her some clothes. This time, she let her mom help her dress. I could hear her mom crying, and I knew her crying would make it worse for Cassie. So, I stepped around where they were, "Here, let me help Cassie dress," I said, looking at her mom.

"Mama, I'm going to be alright. It's just some bruises. They'll go away."

4

LUCA

"Damn it, Cassie, stop. You're going to hurt yourself. You can't do this for so many hours. Stop it." I was worried because Cassie was working herself to death. She had to slow down.

"But I have to get stronger. I have to be able to defend myself."

I heard someone walk up to where we were outside. I knew it was her grandfather. "He's right, Cassie. You're going to hurt yourself. You're going to make it worse. You've only been home for two months. You don't have to do everything at once. Listen to Luca. He knows what he's talking about."

"I'm sorry, of course, you're right. I mean, you must have another life besides taking care of me and teaching me how to fight. Do you have a steady girlfriend?" she asked, not looking me in the eye.

"No, I don't have a steady girlfriend. Cassie, I do not have other things to do. I'm here for you, and I won't let you kill yourself. I leave you for twenty minutes, and you're out here doing this. You can't keep lifting weights. Stop for a while.

We are going to work four hours a day and run for two hours. That's all. Your body will break down if you keep going at your current pace."

"What does running have to do with self-defense?"

"Running is a matter of life and death. If you are ever in the position you were in again, you could run if you could get away. By the time I am finished with you, you'll be running twenty miles before you know it. Will I have to watch you twenty-four hours daily, or will you listen to me?"

"I'll listen to you. I'll do what you say. I'm sorry for being such a pain in the ass." She looked at me, and I knew she was pissed. "I hate that motherfucker. I want to kill him. He killed his grandmother. He said she thought she was the boss, but he showed her. That was her house we were at."

I shook my head. I wished Cassie could stop thinking about that bastard for a while. Sometimes she would remember something from her time there. "I'll call the police and have them check to see about the grandmother," Grandpa said as he walked across the room.

Cassie's chin shook. I knew she was having a bad day remembering things. "Did they ever find out how many women he killed?" she asked.

"I talked to your dad yesterday, and he said they've found six bodies buried on the property."

"I'm ready to go home. I haven't even seen my nephew. I miss Sara. Are you ready to go home?"

"I'm ready when you are."

"Okay. We'll leave on Monday. I'm going to shower." I watched her walk away. I loved Cassie Rossi. I knew she'd break my heart, but my heart was already breaking. I don't think Cassie will ever allow herself to fall in love with a man. But if she does, I'm going to be there, and it will be me.

Every day, it was harder to be near her. Teaching her

self-defense, I had to be touching her daily. And it was getting harder and harder to hide my feelings from her. I didn't care if she broke my heart. It would be worth it if we were together for a little while. Sure, the longer, the better. I'll take whatever I can get.

Grandpa came back into the room. I looked at him. "She's ready to go home. She wants to leave on Monday.

"I'll go with you. I want to see that great-grandbaby of mine. Serena is already there. I'm sure Dante will want to go with us. I'll call him right now."

I walked outside, sat in a lounge chair, and closed my eyes. I only needed to meditate for a little while. It always helped me.

I decided to take a nap. When I woke up, Cassie was sitting in the other lounge chair with her eyes closed. "Are you sleeping?" I asked softly. I didn't want to wake her if she was asleep.

"No, I'm just meditating, the way you showed me. It actually works really well. I can close my eyes and lose myself."

And then she opened those beautiful emerald green eyes and looked at me. "Will you make love with me tonight?"

I sat up straight at that. Did I hear her right? She stared at me for a while before I could say anything. Finally, I asked, "Cassie, are you sure?"

"I've been waiting for you to make a move and you still haven't. I was in the shower earlier and made my mind up; since you haven't made a move, I decided I would. Life is short, Luca. Why not do what you want to do?"

"Damn, you're getting me all worked up, and your grandpa will be coming out here any minute."

"He won't be coming out here. He went to town."

I got up, took her hand, and pulled her up. "Let's not wait until tonight. I'm ready to make love to you right now."

"You are. Okay. I'm ready too."

"You sure?"

"Yes, I am." I took her hand, and I walked her down to my room. I slowly undressed her. I looked at her beautiful body. *Damn, she's mine.*

My hands trailed down her body, which was nothing but muscle now. Her nipples were standing straight. I've bent and put one in my mouth. My tongue licked the other one. I trailed my hand down between her thighs. Then I picked her up and put her on the bed. I took my clothes off and lay naked beside her.

"You're beautiful, baby. Do you know how much I want you?"

"Is it as much as I want you?"

"I've been fighting it since I saw you running down that hill; when I picked you up, it was like time stopped still, and we were back in that cottage in Ireland. I almost bent my head and kissed you right then. That would have shocked everyone."

She chuckled. "What are you talking about? You did kiss me." It was the first chuckle I'd heard from her since I found her in that house. I would spend my life making her laugh if she let me. My hand slipped between her thighs and inside her wetness.

"Yes, but the kiss was so quick it didn't count."

"That's so good. Yes, Luca, you make me forget everything," Cassie cried.

My fingers worked faster. Cassie screamed my name into my neck as she orgasmed. Over and over, she orgasmed then I pushed myself inside her. I went slow at first until she got over her orgasms. Then I went fast. She was almost crying as she orgasmed again. I waited until I knew she was finished, and then I let myself orgasm. We both lay there breathing hard. I was still hard.

"The next time won't be as fast. My body wasn't in control. I'll be in control next time," I said as Cassie pulled herself closer to me, and I kissed her neck.

"Next time, are you kidding me? I'm still having orgasms from the first time. That was so good. I haven't made love since I was with you in Ireland."

I pushed myself against Cassie so she could feel how ready I was for her. I didn't want to scare her. I kissed her and pulled her against me. When she went to sleep, I got up. I called her father to see if he was going with us to Oregon.

"Yeah, I'll go with you. I need to visit the baby before we start harvesting the grapes. When the grapes are ready to pick, there isn't a moment's rest for anyone."

"I'll call the airport," I said, walking onto the balcony. I saw Marlon, Cassie's grandfather, walking into the house. I turned and looked at Cassie lying in bed. She was uncovered. I put the sheet on her and left the room.

"How is our girl?"

"She's sleeping right now. Marlon, do you think she needs to talk to someone."

"No, you are the only someone she needs. I hear her talking to you about her kidnapping. Since she tells you everything, she doesn't need anyone else. Maria has already called the airport, so you don't have to."

"Thank you, I was just going to do that." I sometimes forget how wealthy this family is. Cassie's family has people who take care of most things for them.

"I'm going to call Sara and have her not question Cassie.

I think the more people who don't talk about it with her the better she will be. She doesn't want or need people staring at her, wondering if she will break any minute. I think I did that the first week she was back. One time she told me to stop staring at her. That's how I figured it out."

5

CASSIE

I was a little scared to face Sara. I shouldn't have been, though. When she saw me, she hugged me and kissed my cheek. Then she put the baby in my arms. I looked down at the most beautiful baby I had ever seen. His eyes stared at me, and then he shut them and was asleep.

"He sleeps a lot. I have to force myself not to hold him while he's sleeping and awake. He has yours and Daddy's green eyes. What do you think?"

I looked at my sister. "I love him so much. He's beautiful. I would never want to put him down, either. I'm sure I would stare at him to ensure everything was working perfectly."

"Yes, that's what I do. I don't like him being in his room. He sleeps in our room where we can keep an eye on him."

"What's his name?"

"Now that everyone is here, I'll tell you his name. We named him Ethan Dante Sullivan. We call him Baby Dante," Sara said, looking at her dad.

"Thank you for such an honor, darling. You too, Ethan. Both of you have made me so happy."

"I think that is a perfect name for this little guy. Baby Dante, you are so handsome. Your Aunt Cassie loves you so much."

"I'm going to run over to my house. I'll see all of you later," Luca said, and my heart started beating fast. I almost panicked.

I looked at Luca, "Where do you live?"

"A few miles from here on Ocean Way."

"Thank you for everything. I could never thank you enough for saving me. Are you coming back?"

He pulled me into his arms and kissed me while everyone watched us. "Do you want to go with me?" Luca whispered, with his forehead resting on mine.

"I'll visit here for a while. Then I'll go to your house."

"Call me, and I'll pick you up." I nodded and stepped back. He gave me a quick kiss and told everyone goodbye. I refused to be embarrassed because Luca kissed me. I walked down the hall and into my room. I stopped because it had a crib in it.

Sara walked in behind me. "Cassie, I'm sorry, I changed rooms with you. Mine was too small for a husband and child. Are you angry with me?"

"No, I'm not angry. I don't blame you. I would have done the same thing. I'm going to shower and rest for a while."

"I told Ethan you wouldn't mind. This house is half yours. Please don't think I would ever try changing that."

"I would never think that. I don't want you to worry about me. I'm still a little shaken over what happened. The least of my worries is the size of my bedroom."

"I love you, Cassie. If you need me for anything, all you have to do is tell me."

"Sara, I'm fine. I promise. You don't have to worry about me."

When I got out of the shower, I felt like I needed to get away from everyone. I wrote a note to Sara and explained that I needed to find myself: 'I know that sounds silly. I'm sorry to leave like this. I knew you would talk me out of going. I'm leaving a message for Luca. Can you please give it to him? Always remember, I love you and that wonderful baby boy. I might love Luca too. That's why I'm doing this. I'll never know if it's because he saved me or if I really love him. Okay, that's enough of my rambling.'

I walked outside and climbed into my SUV, not knowing where I was going, but I had to find the Cassie I used to be. The funny girl who laughed all the time, I wanted her back. I knew this before today. But when Luca said he was going home, I felt my body panic. I couldn't depend on Luca to keep me safe. I couldn't continue being afraid to live without Luca standing next to me forever.

6

LUCA

"What are you saying? Did you say Cassie went away? Where did she go?"

"Here, she left you a note."

I took the piece of paper and walked back out to my vehicle. I sat down and opened the small note that Cassie had left for me. 'Luca, I don't want to leave, but I have to find Cassie again. I can't depend on you to take care of me. When you went home, I panicked. I don't like myself doing that. I have to get over this on my own, I can't do that with you taking care of me. I want to be that funny happy woman I used to be.'

Damn it. I knew I should have taken her with me. I saw the panic in her eyes. I know exactly what she's talking about. She doesn't know she is still that person. It takes time to let go of that shit she was subjected to. She went through hell. Doesn't she realize it takes time to overcome the horror she experienced? *My heart hurts*. This is why I never wanted to fall in love. I was glad I didn't tell her I loved her. *I will give her some time, but she will be back and with me.*

LUCA

∼

I LOOKED at Hutch Campbell like he was crazy. I don't know who was worse, him or his brother, Gray. I went to school with both of them from the age of ten. Hutch was a year ahead of me, and Gray was a year behind me. Before that, I went to school for four years in Maine, where I got to know all of the Army Rangers. I even got into fights with them when we were young. I would play football on the beach with the Rangers. We used to spend our summers in Maine. When I got older, I lived with my grandmother here in Oregon most of the time. My grandmother had this beautiful old Victorian home that was now mine.

Gray and his wife, Gilly, had a Victorian home as well. They also had a large shipyard. Gray spent his time off from SEAL Security helping Gilly and their friend Joe, who used to own the shipyard working on the boats. He was almost ninety years old now. I was surprised he took the time to run on the beach with us.

Twenty miles was what we ran. Sometimes more. I wondered if Cassie kept up with the daily workouts and twenty-mile run. She'd been gone for a while now. I decided to look for her if she didn't return within four months. She still had two months to go.

I missed her like hell. I would ask Ethan if they had heard from her, but he always said no. I was surprised because Cassie and Sara were so close. I wondered if she was in Italy visiting her parents and grandfather. But Sara said they would tell her if that's where she went.

"We leave tomorrow for Afghanistan, so be prepared for a long trip," Hutch said as he returned to his place. I saluted him. Hutch has always treated us like we were his kids to boss around. We, in turn, ignored him to a certain point.

We all knew how dangerous this trip was. It went without saying that all of us could die sneaking into Afghanistan to rescue some of our friends who were left behind. I looked at Gray, "Are you going to work on the boat anymore today?" Gray had fallen in love with one of the wrecked boats. It belonged to Joe's brother, who died when he was twenty-one, seventy-five years ago.

"Only for a few hours. Do you feel up to sanding some wood down?"

"Yes, I need to stay busy. And the house is spotless."

"Hey, anytime you want to do some sanding, come over and start. You don't need to wait for me to ask you. It'll take a while to get my boat as I want it anyway and I appreciate all the help I can get."

When we walked onto the boatyard property, Gilly was there, working on the mechanics of the boats. "Hey, sweetheart, we have help sanding today."

"Great, I sold Linda today. So, I'm working on her. Do you think we can work on it instead of yours today?"

"Sure, we can. What do you say, Luca? Do you feel like sanding down this big thing?"

"Sure. It doesn't matter which boat I'm sanding as long as it keeps me busy. Who bought this big old boat?"

"Dante Rossi, it's a surprise for his wife. He wants to give it to her for their anniversary. We have three months to get it going."

"Three months, sweetheart. We can't get this thing done in three months."

"I've hired some teenage boys to help work on it."

"What teenage boys?"

"Just some that I see hanging around."

"Did you hire the Bandura boys?"

"All they need is something to keep them busy. We don't

know if they're bad boys. If we could keep them busy and they can make themselves some money, we can get our boat sanded faster."

"I hope you know what you're doing."

"Gray, of course, I know what I'm doing."

I grabbed the sander, climbed inside the boat and started sanding. I didn't even know what time it was until I saw the sun going down. I looked over at Gray and laughed. He had sand all over himself.

"Don't laugh. You look worse than I do. Have you heard anything from Cassie?" He looked like he felt sorry for me.

"No, I'll give her another month. If she's not back by then, I'll hunt for her. I know she talks to someone in her family. I don't know if she tells them she's alright or if they know where she's at and not telling me. Don't worry about me. Cassie will return."

"Maybe she doesn't want to be found."

"Maybe, but I have to know either way."

"I wish you luck with Cassie."

"Thanks. I'm going to head home. I'll see you at five in the morning."

"Yep, I'll see you then."

I went home thinking about Cassie. She was all I thought about anymore. I picked up the phone, and I called her grandfather.

"Hello."

"Hey, Marlon, it's Luca. I was calling to see if you have heard from Cassie."

"Hello, Luca. She called me and said she was doing fine. I asked her yesterday when she will return to her family, and she said she has an obligation that she has to fulfill and that she will let me know."

"If she's not back in a month, I'm going after her."

"Do you think Cassie would like that? I'm not sure if that's a good idea. I'm her grandfather, and I worry about her just like you. But she's trying to find who she was before that bastard got her. I'll tell her to call you. Let me tell you a story about when my wife died. After Gracie died, I felt like I no longer existed. Sometimes I still have that feeling."

"We fell in love when we were in high school. It's always been Gracie and me. It will never be anyone else. We were both sixteen when we got together. Gracie died when she was fifty-three, from cancer. I didn't know what to do with myself. I loved that woman more than life itself. I blamed the world for taking her away from me. I've never told this story to anyone.

"I bought myself a boat, you see. I planned to go to sea and let the waves take me down. I wanted to be in a place where no one could rescue me. The sea took me down. I swear I was smiling, and then Gracie pulled me up. She was so angry at me. She threw my ass back into that boat and pushed it to the shore. I'm going to trust you not to tell anyone that story. I'll deny it."

"You have my word. Your secret is safe with me. I'm leaving for Afghanistan in the morning. If you talk to her, please ask her to call me. I wanted to hear her voice before I left."

"I'll tell her. Why are you going there?"

"We are rescuing some of our friends who couldn't get out."

"You be careful, Luca. That's a very dangerous place for anyone to go."

"Marlon, I'm sorry about your Gracie. I bet she was an amazing person."

"Yes, she was the best. Our love was once in a lifetime."

"That's how I feel, but don't tell Cassie I said that, or I'll have to deny it."

He chuckled. "My lips are sealed. I won't say a word."

7

CASSIE

I didn't plan on staying gone this long. I sat down and called grandpa before I left for work.

"Sweetheart, I just got off the phone with Luca. He's heading to Afghanistan early in the morning to rescue some of their friends who couldn't get out when the United States left that country. He said he would love to hear from you before he leaves. Why don't you give him a call?"

"Grandpa, how is everyone? I'll call Luca before I go to bed."

"Everyone is good. We will be going to Oregon for Christmas this year. I hope you will be there."

"I'll do my best. I still have to finish what I'm doing. I love you, Grandpa."

"I love you too, sweetie. I can't wait to see you. Cassie, if you need anything, I'll make it happen. All you have to do is tell me what you need."

"I know you will, Grandpa. But I'm fine. I'm busy working. I signed up to do three months in India, so here I am. Tell everyone I'm fine. As soon as I finish my time here, I'll be home. Goodbye, Grandpa."

LUCA

"Goodbye, honey."

I took a deep breath and called Luca. It rang so many times, I was about to hang up when he answered.

"This better be good. I was in the shower."

I giggled. "I wish I was in that shower with you."

"Sweetheart, I wish you were here with me too. I miss you. I need you to call me, I worry about you. You know I'm a worrier."

"I miss you too. I'll be home before you get back from your next job. Please be careful while you are in Afghanistan."

"I will, sweetheart. Where are you?"

"I'm in India, working at a teaching hospital. I'll be back home when I've finished this job."

"I can't wait to see you. How did you get to India?"

"I took a plane."

"I mean, what made you decide to go to India?"

I chuckled. "I know, sorry. They were short on nurses. I signed a contract to work here for three months."

"How are you, sweetheart?"

"I'm better. I don't want you worrying about me. I've come to a few conclusions since I've been here without you. And the most important thing is that life is short and we need to live each day as if it's our last. And what I want is to be in your life."

"I want you in my life. I want you to be with me always. Tell me how India is."

"I haven't been doing much here except working, so most of my time is spent in the hospital. I have a little apartment around the corner from work. It's different than the United States. But, I have been going to other countries as a traveling nurse, so I'm used to different things. The people are very kind."

"Promise me you'll stay safe."

"I'm not going to do anything crazy. I miss you so much. I wish you were here. When are you going to Afghanistan?"

"We leave in a couple of hours. All we have to do is go in there and get our friends out and then we're coming straight home. I hope you're here when I get back. Cassie, take care of yourself.

"I'm sorry for worrying you and my family. It felt like everybody was smothering me and staring at me, wondering if I would break down in front of them. I'm going to be fine. I'm going to forget about that bastard. It wasn't even about me. It was about the other women who died, the ones who that fucker raped. I'm lucky I came out alive. Let's not talk about him anymore. From now on, our life goes forward. We're not going to look backward in that rearview mirror."

"I agree, sweetheart. We'll only go forward."

"I have to go now. I have to be at work in ten minutes. I'll see you next month."

"OK, sweetheart, I'll see you next month."

When I hung up the phone, I smiled. I knew my life was going to be wonderful from here on out. I loved Luca, and he loved me. *We're going to have a family together. We're going to raise our kids to know they are loved. Our kids can play with Sara's kids as we did our entire lives. I'll call Sara when I get off work.*

Not everyone liked it when I came to work in India. Some people thought I was taking someone else's job away from them. And all I was doing was filling in for them while they went on vacation. I tried explaining it to people who would come into the hospital talking about me to everyone who would listen. There are people in this world that thrive on arguing with others.

I smiled as I entered the hospital. The girl at the reception desk was ready to have her baby in another month. She and her husband were excited about the baby. I would be excited if it were me. I smiled, watching her. "How's mom and baby feeling?"

"We feel wonderful. Thank you for asking. You're going to have a busy day today. There was a big car pileup on the freeway. The emergency room is packed."

"I better get in there and help the doctors." I put my bag away and rushed to the E.R. People were everywhere. The difference between the United States and here was that there was always chaos here in the emergency room. But they knew what they were doing. What looked like chaos to me was proficient for the lead nurse.

"Thank goodness you are here. There are people in rooms ten, eleven, and sixteen. Take your pick."

I walked to room ten, and two kids were crying while their mom was lying on the gurney. She looked to be unconscious. I started working on her and looked over at the kids. "Do you want to call your daddy?"

"Yes."

"Tell me his number." I thought I should be the one to call their dad. The kids were still crying. "Hello, I'm a nurse at the teaching hospital in the emergency room. There was an accident, and your wife has been injured. Your boys wanted to call you." I answered a few questions and handed the phone to the boys. They talked for a few minutes, then handed me the phone back.

I had just checked out her head wound when the doctor walked in. He said something to the kids, and then he looked at me. "Cassie, what have we got here?"

"She has a head wound, and I saw blood on the back of her dress. The boy's father is on his way here. I'll take the boys out and be right back." I took the boys to the nurse's station and told them not to leave.

When I returned to the room, the doctor had already turned the woman over and checked her back. I couldn't help the gasp when I saw her injury. She had a big chunk missing from her back.

"She's going to have surgery. The boys can stay at the nurse station until their father gets here. Can you go to room sixteen? They have three patients there."

"Yes, doctor, I'll go right now." They put more people in room sixteen because it was larger. When I entered, nurse Anna was there. She looked like she was crying. "Anna, are you okay?"

"Yes, this girl is my cousin. I called my aunt and uncle, and they were both crying. Her baby didn't make it. She was eight months pregnant. Her husband is on his way."

I started working on the other woman. She was awake and looked at me.

"I want to go home. I'm not hurting that much."

"You have to stay here until the doctor says you can go home. Let me check you out; where are you hurting?"

"My leg has a cut on it, and my arm is broken. When my parents get here, we'll tell them I'm fine. They get scared when something happens to their children, and I'm the baby in the family."

"Well, Penny, you need to get your arm x-rayed. I'll have an orderly come and get you. If your parents show up before you return, I'll tell them you're fine and only getting your arm X-rayed."

"Thank you."

"You're welcome." I walked over to the next patient. He was lying there staring at me. I smiled at him. "How are you feeling?" He didn't answer me. So, I asked him again, "How are you feeling? Can you hear what I'm saying? Penny, have you checked this patient out?"

"I haven't had time. I'm still with my cousin."

"I think he's in shock." I worked for ten minutes before his eyes registered that I had said something.

Thirteen hours later, I was walking home. My mind drifted to Luca and I wondered how he was doing. I wondered if he was already in Afghanistan or if they had to stop somewhere else. I forgot to ask him all those questions.

When I got home, I called Sara. She texted me pictures of her and the baby, even some of Ethan and the baby. Then she texted me a picture of Luca holding her baby. And his eyes went wide as he realized the baby was pooping. I laughed so hard. *Oh, I miss my family. I can't wait to see them again.*

8

LUCA

I looked over at Ryker as we started to land. "Who's going to stay with the airplane?"

"Leo is staying. We need to get in and out of here as fast as possible. I'm not even sure where those people are hiding. We'll follow the map. We'll get them, and we'll come right back here. I don't want anybody to be shot at."

"I don't want that either. I plan on having a long, happy life." I watched Ryker sticking knives in his boots. He had two guns, and a hatchet hooked to his belt. I looked at the other guys. Hell, they were all loaded up too. I shrugged my shoulders, adjusted my dark hoody, grabbed the few knives I carried, and put them in my boots.

I grabbed another gun and tucked it into the waistband of my pants. I prayed we wouldn't get caught. All the lights on the airplane were off. We couldn't have lights of any kind. We were in a flat desert. Any light could be detected.

"Let's go."

We followed the map and went south. All of us could run for miles. We'd been running for about three hours when we heard a noise.

"Get down," I hissed. We lay in the sand and listened. God, I hope we weren't on the road. There was so much sand out here, and I couldn't tell if this was a road or just sand on the side of the road.

We saw the lights. It looked like they were coming straight at us. We rolled down a little slope. I prayed they would turn. Music was blasting from the jeep. It was like they didn't even care if someone heard it. We kept our heads down and they drove past us.

I hoped they weren't going to the airplane. If they were, we couldn't beat them back there. "I wish our radios worked out here so I could call Leo and tell him to get out of the airplane," I whispered as we watched them drive down the road, getting further and further away.

Jackson looked over at me. "If he sees headlights coming, he'll leave the plane. Leo knows what to do. He's been on this route too often to not know what to do. He'll see the lights and get the hell out of there."

"That's true. We started back running. How many people are we saving?" I asked because I had forgotten to ask before.

"Eight, five men and three women. The Army Rangers will be here next week picking some up. I can't believe we ran off and left everybody here. And we're still finding them."

"Thank God for all the people who risk their lives to find them. I'm not talking about us. I'm talking about all the injured servicemen and women who continually come back here to save the people who they said they would save. They use their own money trying to get their friends out of here," Blade Wilder said.

We knew not to get Blade started. We're all angry because of how the government pulled out of Afghanistan.

A lot of our friends that were left behind died. Blade had a cousin who died over here. He came here to rescue some people, got shot down, and died. We were all in shock. That's why you don't say anything to Blade about the administration clearing out Afghanistan as fast as it did. The Taliban wouldn't give his cousin's body back to his family. Blade went a little crazy trying to return his cousin's body to America. They said they buried his body and didn't know where it was buried.

We saw a big explosion and knew it was our airplane. I prayed that Leo got out before it blew up. "Now, how are we going to get out of here?" I asked, watching the ball of fire in the sky.

"Fuck if I know. I don't see other airplanes lying around waiting for us. Let's get the people, and then we'll worry about how we'll get home," Ryker said, picking up speed. We all started to run faster. I was glad I had worked out with Cassie teaching her self-defense. We all had to keep up with our physical fitness because sometimes we had a lot of life-or-death hands-on contact.

"I guess you know they'll be hunting us down because they know that plane didn't get here on its own," I said, looking at the others. "We have to find a place to stay before the sun comes up or we will be caught red-handed. So, if you see a building in the distance, we'll check it out."

The sun was rising, and we were still running when we saw dust approaching us. "Fuck. Be ready to fire," I shouted. We all took our stance and waited. When the jeep came over the hill, Leo called out as he stood in his seat and held his gun up.

We all laughed. When he came to a stop, we all hit him on the back. "One more hit and I'll take this jeep back. We no longer have a plane, but maybe there is another rescue, and we can catch a ride with them. We'll keep our fingers crossed that someone else is here."

"I hope to hell they are. I don't want to stay longer than we have to. The Rangers are supposed to come next week, and we can catch a ride with them. Tell us how you got off that plane."

"I saw the light from far away. I wasn't sure if you all were still alive. I hid behind the plane's wheel when they went inside the plane. I rolled the jeep far enough away that they didn't pay any attention to it. I shot them when they were jumping and laughing because the plane blew up."

"Let's get in the jeep. We'll find the people, and then we'll find a plane to take us home," Ryker said. "If we don't make it home, Gabby will be pissed."

I silently prayed we would make it home. "We've been in worse situations than this. We'll rescue those we came to rescue and find a way out of here. Now, I'm going to shut my eyes for a moment," I said as I got comfortable in the front seat. I woke up when we hit a pothole.

"Damn," I looked around. "Did you hit that hole on purpose?"

"What hole? I didn't see anything. Sorry if I woke you. We're entering a place where there are some buildings. We need to find a place to park until it gets dark, and then we'll get back on the road."

We found a run-down building with a garage door that the jeep could fit inside. It also had stairs that went to the roof. "All of you can get some sleep. I'll be on the lookout first," I said, climbing the stairs up to the roof. The building looked like it had been shot up pretty badly. That was fine; we only needed it for a while.

I sat in a chair up there, and my thoughts went to Cassie. I hoped she stayed safe. I couldn't wait to see her. I tried to stay low so I wouldn't be seen, but I had to keep an eye on the horizon. I was standing behind what looked like a stack to a pot belly stove. I figured it was put here for just this reason—so you could see if anyone was coming.

"Do you see anything?" Jackson asked.

"No, nothing. I wonder why they put all of these buildings out here."

"Who knows? I imagine their army lived here at one time so that they could watch for people coming into their country. This would be the perfect spot to trap your enemy."

"You're right. I can see everywhere from here. Why don't you get some shut-eye, and I'll keep an eye out for the bad guys," Jackson said, walking around the roof.

We ensured nothing was around when we started the jeep up and left. The stars were bright. We were on the road for a few hours when we saw the lights around us. Bullets started flying, and we all jumped out of the jeep, firing our guns. I saw Ryker fly back when a bullet hit him. I grabbed him and pulled him away from the jeep.

"Fuck! Kill these bastards!" I roared. "We have to save Ryker. Mother fuckers!" I turned and started shooting. I walked toward them like a crazy man. I'm sure they thought I was crazy, walking toward them instead of running. I was six-three, and I wouldn't back down. Ryker had a baby that needed him home alive. I wouldn't let him die.

"They're turning around. You scared the hell out of them!" Leo shouted. I ran back to Ryker; Jackson had already ripped his shirt off. I looked at his chest where the bullet hit him and saw the chain with all their pictures on that big piece of metal. It had a big dent in the center, and the bullet was stuck in the piece of metal where those pictures were. "It didn't penetrate his skin. The necklace he wore saved his life. I will never again tease him about his necklace."

I tapped him on the face until he opened his eyes. "Tell my family I love them more than anything. Tell Gabby I'm so sorry."

I chuckled. "You tell them when we get back home."

"What?" Ryker bent and looked at his chest.

"You'll have a big bruise, but your necklace saved your life."

"I told you this was my lucky necklace. The damn bullet is stuck in my necklace. We have to get it out before Gabby sees this. I have to get this fixed before she sees it. She'll have a fit and make me quit my job."

"Are you pussy whipped?"

"Don't even go there, Luca, until you have a wife and children."

"Ok, I'm sorry I said that. Hey, I'm just glad you are alive."

"Yeah, you should have seen Luca; he turned around and started charging those men while shooting both guns. They took off running. Luca looked like a madman charging and roaring as loud as he could."

"I was pissed because I didn't want to tell Gabby you died. It scared me to death thinking about talking to her."

"Yeah, I'm glad you don't have to. It would have destroyed her."

I slapped Ryker on the back and grabbed his hand to help him stand. "Let's get going. They'll be back once they realize we are still here with one of their jeeps."

We had traveled for maybe twenty miles when I noticed something I had seen on the map. "Wait, stop here. Isn't this the place where we are supposed to pick them up?" I asked, pulling the map out of my backpack. "Turn here." We drove for thirty minutes and looked around. "It has to be this building." We got out of the jeep and walked behind the building. I rapped on the door three times. It was opened slowly.

I looked at the man and smiled. "Kash, what are you doing here?"

"We came to rescue one of our guys. He's here locked up somewhere. They told us to come here, and we'll find out where he is. What are you doing here?"

"We are supposed to pick up eight people who were left behind because of that stupid departure from here. This doesn't feel right. I think we all need to get the hell out of this building."

"I agree." We jumped into the jeep and left. Kash and a couple of the Army Rangers followed us in their jeep. We drove until we found an empty house where we could figure out what was going on.

"Who does the Taliban have?"

"They have Asher Wright. We have to find him before they kill him."

"We'll help you find him and ride home with you guys since they blew up our airplane. They lured us here to kill us. They must be on to us, but how did they get our phone number? I talked to the person who called us. He sounded American, but that doesn't mean anything anymore."

"Yeah, the guy I talked to was also American. I mean, he sounded American. Ruby will not be happy if I don't bring him back. If she weren't pregnant, she would have been here with us. She is not someone who takes no for an answer."

"I took out my goggles and scanned the area. Here they come. Okay, as soon as nightfall arrives, we'll head out to look for Asher. Why was he here alone?"

"He wasn't alone. But they had to leave him because they

had twenty-four women and babies. The babies are starving over here. We couldn't wait any longer for him. The Taliban were right on our tail. We had to leave."

"Sometimes, the only choices you have to make are not the ones you want to make." We watched as the Taliban left after shooting up the building. "They are going to keep looking for us. We need to move as soon as we can."

"Luca, check this out."

I walked over to where Jackson and the others stood, looking down at a little boy lying on the floor. Anger pushed to the front of my mind, and then I saw his arm move. I bent and picked him up. "I wonder where his mother is."

"That man took her," the little boy said, wiping his eyes as tears started to fall.

"What's your name?"

"My name is Frank, and I'm five. My grandpa's name is Frank too. We were going to go to Grandpa's but we got caught. Mommy said to stay hidden until someone nice finds me. Are you nice?"

"Yeah, I'm nice. Where does your grandpa live?"

"He lives in America. The mean men shot my daddy. Now I don't have a daddy." Large tears landed on his cheeks, and I held him closer to me, and he laid his head on my shoulders. "Can we find Mommy now?"

"We'll try and find your mommy. You will stay with us, and we'll take you to your grandpa. If we find your mom, we'll take her with us too. Let's feed you. Stay close to us, and don't wander off."

"Okay."

I carried him to my pack and gave him some jerky and a granola bar. Then I poured some water for him into my cup. He would not let go of my hand. "You can let go of my hand now." I looked at him, and another tear fell.

"Everyone here is a nice person. You don't have to be afraid."

"I want to stay with you."

What the hell do I do now? I looked at Jackson, who gave me a dirty look. He knew what I was going to do. He had always said kids hate him but their mommies love him. I would prove him wrong, starting with this kid.

"Frank, this is Jackson. He will stay near you. He is a nice man who will keep you safe." Frank frowned at Jackson.

"Do you like kids?"

"Of course, I like kids."

"Do you have any kids?"

"No, I don't have any children."

"Okay, I'll stay near you because you like kids."

"Good, grab your jerky and follow me." I watched as the little boy followed behind Jackson, trying to take giant footsteps. I chuckled as I returned to where Kash was talking to a couple more Rangers.

"What happened with the little boy?"

"They took his mommy, but she hid him before they saw him. She's American. We'll keep our eyes out for her as well."

9

LUCA

I couldn't believe we'd already been here for three weeks waiting for someone to pick us up. Each time, it'd been a false message. So now we were out on our own, we'd do the finding and the rescuing. We weren't listening to anyone else. Hopefully, we would find Asher and the boy's mother.

Frank would not let Jackson out of his sight. Most of the time, he was on Jackson's back. We'd been doing a lot of walking. Thank God the Rangers could run as far in a day as we could. Both of our Jeeps ran out of fuel. For now, we were walking. The nights were cold, and the days hot. I just wanted to get the hell out of this damn sandpile.

All I could think of was Cassie. I hoped she was home. We'd heard stories about a large earthquake in India. I hoped to hell Cassie was safe. It was late at night. "Let's get ready to find a place to sleep..." we heard voices talking.

"Who the hell is that?" I said, turning around with my hand up to stop all the talking.

I held up my hand at the same time that Kash did his. We crawled closer to the group to see if we could understand what they were saying and if they had any prisoners. One thing we found out is that they were laughing about tricking us.

I thought I heard him talking about the Americans that they had. I wondered if it was Frank's mom or maybe even Asher. Perhaps they had two prisoners. Kash and I crawled in the sand so we could get closer. I saw the woman. She was making them a plate of food. I didn't know if they abused her, but she needed to be gotten out of there.

We both nodded. We counted the men. There were about twelve of them that we could see. I let out a roar, and every one of them jumped up. Jackson kept Frank safe while we fought the men. I saw the woman running. She must have seen her little boy. One guy told us he would tell us where Asher was if we didn't kill him. We let him live.

I was happy we found Frank's mother. She told us that the men didn't rape her because her husband was high up in the service, and they didn't want to disrespect that. All we had to do was find Asher, and we would be out of there. We found him three days later. All of us were overjoyed that he was safe. He'd gotten into a few fights, but he was alive. It was time to go home.

We made our way to the plane but had to stop because we ran into another group of Taliban soldiers. They were all over the plane that would take us out of this desert. Now, what were we going to do? We were tired and rundown. Our rations wouldn't last much longer because we shared our food with the others we were with.

"Do you think the Taliban was telling us the truth when he said there was a big earthquake in India," I said, looking at my buddies.

Ryker looked over at me. "I'm sure Cassie is out of there by now. We've been here for a month already. If the earthquake happened two days ago, that still has her out of there. You told me she had three more weeks since you last talked to her."

"Yeah, you're right. I'm sure she's home. Besides, we don't even know how bad the earthquake was. You know how rumors get spread. Rumors get stretched way out of proportion. I'm sure it's not as bad as they said it was. As soon as we get a radio signal, I can call and find out what's happening."

We found a little hiding spot so that the Taliban wouldn't see us, and we had to plan how we would get our plane back. We were tired of fighting, but if it came to that, we'd get into another one. We decided to wait it out and see if they would leave. We couldn't stay around here too long; our food would run out.

We had to ration our water. It was almost all gone as well. So, we only sipped a drink a couple of times a day. We let the child have more than we had because he didn't understand a sip, and we were fine with that.

We took turns sleeping. We wanted to make sure the Taliban couldn't see us. We mostly did hand signals or whispered. We didn't want them to overhear anything, and your voice carried a long way in the desert.

I wished all of this was over, I wanted Cassie to be home safe, and I could talk to her. I needed to make sure she was home. I felt like going in there and killing every one of those bastards. Someone shook my shoulder, and I opened my eyes. Ryker put his hand over his lips, telling me not to say anything. Then he pointed over my shoulder.

I turned to see what was happening, and the Taliban were leaving. I prayed, hoping we could get out of this place fast. We waited an hour, so they didn't hear the plane when it started.

"Do you think they left anyone on the plane?" I asked, looking over at the others.

"Only one way to find out," Ryker said.

We quietly walked to the plane. And when we got there, Matt, one of the Army Rangers, swung himself over the side quietly. If somebody was on the plane, we did not want them to see us. We would rather surprise them than have them surprise us. We stood out on the ground when a man flew past us. He landed with a hard thump. He was knocked out, but he was alive. Matt found him sitting in the driver's seat of the plane. We let him live.

We were in the air for a few hours when I could make a call. I couldn't get hold of Cassie, so I called her grandfather. It took a while for him to answer. "Hello."

"Hello, Luca, is this you?"

"Yes, I want to know where Cassie is?"

"She was still in India when the earthquake hit. We can't get hold of her. She must have dropped her phone. Dante and Serena are there. I can't get hold of them. I'm going to be leaving to go there also. They probably don't have any internet right now. Where are you?"

"I'm just leaving Afghanistan. Why don't you wait, and I'll meet you in Italy before you take off? That way, I can ride with you."

"Okay, I'll wait for you. Don't be too long. If she's lost somewhere, I want to help find her."

"I'm sure she's not lost. She's probably helping people. You know how Cassie is. She always does stuff like this. She jumps in without thinking. She's probably down in all that rubble, digging people out of there. Please, if you hear anything, let me know."

"I will. How was Afghanistan?"

LUCA

"It was a trap. We figured it out in time before they trapped us. I'll tell you about it when I see you."

"Okay, I'll see you then. I'll be at the airport waiting for you."

I ran my hands down my face. It was full of whiskers and filth. I would love a shower, but that would have to wait. The main thing right now was Cassie. I smiled and shook my head.

I told the guys what was going on. They decided to go with me to India. We agreed that the Rangers would drop us off in Italy and then head home. And we would find Cassie and bring her home. I knew she was lost deep inside those fallen buildings, but I tried to chase that thought away. I didn't want it to bring bad luck to Cassie. But it nagged at my mind and wouldn't leave.

I must have dozed off. When I opened my eyes, we were landing. I looked at my friends and teammates. "You don't have to do this. I could look for her. It's not safe. I doubt if you will get any good meals?"

"Hey, that's our life. We help our brothers. We are not going home while you go alone to India to dig in the rubble, hunting for Cassie. We know you would be there for us, and we will always be there for you."

"I know. You guys are always there for me. And I will be there for you too. Thank you for going with me."

"You're welcome. Now let's get ready and go. So, where's Grandpa going to meet us?"

"He will be at the airport somewhere." We were stepping off the plane when we heard somebody. I raised my head and looked over. Grandpa was standing next to the shiny new plane waving. "There he is. Thanks for the ride, Kash and Matt. We'll see you guys around."

"You can be sure of it. Take care of yourselves. I hope you find your lady," Kash said.

Grandpa stood waving us over to him. I was shocked when I realized I loved this old man. We ran over to where he stood. "I hope we find her soon. Have you talked to Serena or Dante?" I said, taking his arm as we walked onto the plane.

"No, I haven't been able to get hold of anybody. The lines are all down. They have no phone or internet. I was hoping they would have called before you landed, and then that way, I could have told you what was happening. But now we'll all have to wait and figure it out when we get there."

"Thanks for waiting for me, Marlon. This will save me a lot of time. I was praying that she would already be at home. I love her more than anything in the world."

"I know you do. We were all hoping she would call and tell us she was safe. Cassie is a very strong woman. You made sure she was physically in shape. She's had to be strong her whole life. She and Sara didn't have it easy. Her life has taught her that she has to take care of herself. One thing about Cassie, she's not lazy."

"She jumps in there and does her job, plus anyone else's if she has extra time on her hands. We were so blessed when we found them girls, or they found us. My life was pretty boring before they came along," he said, patting me on the back. "I ordered food for all of you. So, you can relax and eat your dinner."

"Thank you. We are all starving." He sat beside me; I knew he was as upset as I was.

"Who would have ever thought that their uncles would have kidnapped them, and leave the country and let us believe that they burned to death in the house they caught on fire. That is the most horrific story I've ever heard. And it's a true one. Those boys will be locked up forever. I don't care if they are my son's or not. They let greed take over in their head. And in the meantime, six lives were destroyed. And we were all heartbroken thinking the babies were dead."

"The good thing is that you are all back together again. All we have to do is find Cassie, and everything will be perfect."

"You really believe that everything will be perfect? I have never in my life known life to be perfect, except when my lady and I married. We were just young kids, but we were so much in love. We were blessed to have our daughter, Serena. I wish my wife could have lived forever. But that damn cancer took her away."

I knew he was thinking about Gracie, the love of his life.

"Maybe that's why I think life can never be perfect. Cause there will always be some obstacle in your path."

"I don't know. I think however you want life to be is how it will be. If you are always sad, your life's going to be sad. If you're happy, then your life's going to be happy. I believe how you live your life depends on whether or not you will have a happy or sad life."

"I love Cassie, and I'm going to have a long, happy life with her. I believe that. Now I just have to find her."

"I believe you're right. Now, why are we talking about something so depressing."

"I don't know. Let's change the subject. What has been happening in your life lately?"

"Not much. It's harvest time, so I've been busy making the wine. Why don't you lie back and take a little nap? I'm sure you haven't gotten much rest since you've been gone."

"Thank you," I said.

I was having a nightmare. I dreamed Cassie was under

all that rubble, and I was trying to dig her out. I woke up in a sweat and looked around.

"We'll be there soon. The others have already showered. If you want to take a shower, help yourself."

"You have a shower on your plane?"

He chuckled, and I thought he might be a little embarrassed. But then he said, "Yep, I love my showers. The water's not real warm, but you can take a quick shower."

"Well, I'm glad you do because I would love to shower."

By the time I finished my shower, it was turning light outside, and everyone was awake. I was anxious to get there and find Cassie. Hopefully, she was alright and was helping other people. That's what I prayed for; she was one of the helpers and not one of the people buried in that rubble. I couldn't think about that.

Marlon's phone started ringing. He jumped three feet when that thing went off. I didn't know what the heck was happening. He actually dropped the phone, before picking it up again.

"Hello."

"Dad, it's me, Serena."

"Serena, what is going on there?"

"We can't find her anywhere. The hospital is completely gone. I don't know if she was at the hospital or if she was at her apartment. But the apartment building is still standing. I don't know if Cassie ran out to help other people out of the rubble or what. We looked everywhere. I don't want you to come here because it's just horrible. It's a nightmare."

"We will be landing soon, sweetheart. We are already here. I have Luca and some of his buddies with me."

"Where are you going to land?"

"Where did you land?"

"Okay, Dad, there is a place on the city's outskirts. You're going to have to land there on the east side. The main airstrip is gone. I'm not even sure if they will allow you to land. You're just going to have to talk to them. I'll give you the phone number. Let me talk to Luca."

"She wants to talk to you."

I took the phone and kept it on speaker. "Hello."

"Luca, I don't know what we'll find, but I will tell you right now; I'm not in it anymore. It was just too horrible. I couldn't stay out there with those dead people everywhere. I would run up to them to see if it was my Cassie," she said as she started crying.

"I'm sorry for crying. I'm helping with the babies now. I don't even know where Cassie was. I'm glad you're coming to help. Dante is going crazy. He hasn't even stopped. His hands are bleeding. He gave his gloves to another man. Maybe you can get him to take a break."

"I'll talk to him when we get there. Take care of yourself, Serena. It would help if you didn't get sick. Cassie will need her mom when we find her. Can I ask you, are they saving a lot of people? Are they able to find the people that are under the rubble?"

"Yes, they saved some people that were under there. So, I hope we will find her if she is somewhere in that rubble." I heard a catch in her voice, but she didn't start back crying.

"The hospital, it's like each floor fell on top of the other floor. Layer on layer, but there are big spots where people can crawl out and not be completely squashed under the rubble. I don't even know how else to describe it. I'll see you guys when you get here," Serena said.

I took a deep breath. *It sounds so much worse than I thought. What does she mean by each layer landed on the other layer in the hospital?* I closed my eyes and prayed, asking God to let Cassie be Okay. All I wanted was for her to be safe. *I will build her a completely padded room when I get her home, so she can stop getting into all these messes. I can't understand how she is always in the wrong place at the wrong time.*

I looked at Marlon and I knew he felt the same as me. "Can I ask you a question? I know you only knew Cassie until she was two. But those two years when she walked, did she always get into trouble."

He looked at me, and he laughed out loud. "Cassie started walking when she was seven months. We were all so proud of her, but then we thought we would have to put a harness on Cassie. If she could climb on something, she climbed on it. You could not put a baby's gate up because she would climb over that gate. She could climb over anything."

"She could squeeze between anything. And that's what I keep thinking about. She can climb over anything. She will not let rubble hold her down. She'll find the best holes and anything else she needs to climb out of that damn stuff."

"Thank you so much. That's what I needed to hear. That is exactly what I needed to hear. Because I know she will get out of there. If she's in there, we don't even know if she is in there. If she is, she will get out."

10

CASSIE

The ground didn't shake, it bucked the floor and tossed me up into the air and I landed on my side. I held onto the wall. That's when I realized we were having an earthquake. I shouted for everyone to run out of the building. I was running when the building started falling apart. I got under a desk I spotted and held my hands over my ears. There was so much screaming. I couldn't believe this was happening to us.

I felt something land on the desk, and then I knew nothing. I woke up to cries; people were in pain, and most were stuck where they were. I opened my eyes, and cement dust filled the air around me. I pulled my shirt over my face so that I wouldn't inhale the stuff, I knew it would harm my lungs. But then I thought I hoped I still had the chance to worry about my lungs, and this wasn't the end of my life.

Why am I worried about my lungs when buried under tons of concrete? Damn Cassie hold it together.

The desk was on top of me. I tried moving it, but there was a cement block on it. That's what knocked me out. I laid back with my eyes closed because I didn't want to get any more cement debris and cement powder in them. I could hear people crying, begging for help. I must have blacked out again. When I opened my eyes, I was in the same place. I had hoped that I was having a nightmare.

I felt the back of my head. There was a large knot. This was why I was knocked out. I started spinning and realized another earthquake shook the building. It wasn't as strong as the first one, but all the stuff that had not come down before started coming down. I could barely breathe. There was so much debris in the air.

I couldn't believe this was the way I was going to die. I was stuck under a broken desk with tons of cement on top of it. I didn't do anything except pray. I prayed that there weren't many people who lost their lives or were stuck down here with me. I knew I was on the third floor, so if what I thought happened did happen, we collapsed on top of the second and first floors.

I lay there for hours, afraid to try and move anything. I must have slept because I came to with a jerk. People were screaming in pain. What could I do? *Luca, I need you.*

I tried to move my body. My mind went down my body to see if anything was broken. I didn't believe I had any broken bones. Maybe my foot was under something, and I couldn't move it. I had to get out of here. I shut my mind to the horror going around me. I shut my mind down and meditated as Luca showed me.

I could see what was going on. If I could just wiggle my foot out from under whatever held it so tightly. I had to get out from under this desk to see where I was. I couldn't plan if I didn't know what was going on. But my damn foot was caught on something. So, it looked like I'd be down here for another night.

I woke up and knew that if I had to leave this cement

tomb before I slept again, or I wouldn't leave this place alive. I had no idea if it was night or day. All I could see was darkness. *I have to get out of this building before we have another earthquake. I am not dying here.*

I could hear people crying. "Hello, can you hear me? Hello, can you answer me, please?" I tried talking calmly to them to calm them down. Nothing worked. *They must be in so much pain.* I raised my head and looked around at my predicament. *I have to make a plan.*

I noticed the desk was broken into pieces, so I had to slide out from under it before it completely gave out and crumbled from the weight of the concrete on it. My shoulders were free, and the rest of my body; all except the foot. I could finally turn over to see what was blocking my foot.

It was a medicine cabinet or something. I remembered that I went to get some medicine for my patient.

The damn thing was stuck under the cement, and my foot was under it. I had to break it apart with something. *I have to get my foot out. I have to find a way out of this damn concrete casket. I swear Luca will never ask me to marry him as much trouble as I get into.*

I keep getting into all these messes, but I swear I don't do it intentionally. One day one of these messes will kill me. But I will not let it be this time. I'm healthy, not squashed. I can get out and will. Remember that, Cassie. You're strong!

With my other foot, I started kicking that damn medicine cabinet. When I kicked the cabinet, it hurt my foot. Oh well. No pain, no gain. I had to kick it. I had to get it off my foot. I heard a man saying something. "Hello, can you hear me? I'm right here," I said out loud.

"Where are you? Yes, I can hear you. You've been talking to yourself out loud for hours."

"I'm sorry. I'm stuck. I'm trying to get my foot released

from the medicine cabinet. It landed on my foot. When I get unstuck, then I can help you. Are you stuck?"

"Did you say you are going to help me? We aren't going anywhere unless you're Superman and can lift these big old concrete blocks off us. We're dead, and you know it. You might as well acknowledge it."

That pissed me off. "Hey, I'm not dead until I'm dead. I'm not going to acknowledge anything. I might not be Superman, but at least I will try to get out of this place. Stay there if you want to lie under that big cement block, but I will get out. And I'll tell your family that you gave up. So, you better tell me your name." I was crying and didn't even know it. I was so upset.

"It's Doctor Ahmed, and I know who you are—Cassie Rossi, traveling nurse. Cassie, when you get out, will you tell my wife I love her? And I will love her forever, even if I am in heaven, since you say you will get out of here. I'll leave it to you to tell her."

"Oh my God," I said as I rolled my eyes. *These people have no faith whatsoever.* "Let me get this damn medicine cabinet off my foot, and then I will crawl to where you are, and we will find a way out of here. Can you at least look around and see any little tunnel we can crawl through? Does anyone see any light?"

"Alright. I'll look around if you promise to stop talking for ten minutes. I hope you do get out. As stubborn as you are when we ask you to do something in surgery, it won't surprise me if you get us all out of here."

"How many of you are in here?"

"I'm here. Hello Cassie."

"I'm here. I believe in you, Cassie. Just be careful when kicking so something else doesn't fall on you."

"I'm here."

"I guess I'm here too. So, tell us, Cassie, how will you get us all out of here?"

Oh crap. The one lead nurse that hates me, I will have to save them so she can't write something bad on my report. "Let me get my foot unstuck, and then I will get all of you unstuck and out of here."

Doctor Ahmed chuckled. "Cassie, maybe you shouldn't make promises like that unless you know you can keep them."

"If I say I'm going to do it, then I will do it. One thing I know, you're supposed to say what you believe, and what you believe will then happen. So, I believe I will rescue all of you, and I will."

"Everyone shut up and let her get her foot unstuck," the mean nurse shouted. "I'm here with two dead people, and it is starting to smell."

I gave the cabinet a hard kick, and that helped a lot. So, I kicked it again. When it came unstuck, I looked at my foot. It had a huge gash in it, but I didn't care. I had to get out from under this desk. I saw an opening and crawled out of there.

I saw Band-Aids and antiseptic cream. I grabbed both and put them on my foot. Then I stuffed the rest of them in my pocket. I was sitting up for the first time since the first earthquake.

I started humming to myself as I looked around and saw a tunnel I could fit through, but I needed one big enough for the doctor to fit through. "I wish I had some water."

"Why don't you believe you have some water, and maybe it will appear before you," the mean nurse said, as she giggled.

I chuckled, and when I bent my head, I spotted three

water bottles. I laughed out loud. "I found three bottles of water. I'll keep them with me."

"I think she'll do it," said Deanna, the mean nurse. *Maybe she isn't as mean as I thought she was.*

I had crawled around for a couple of hours when I saw a larger tunnel. I knew the doctor would fit through it. "Hey, I see some light."

"Cassie, follow the light. You can get help for us when you get out. If you have a chance to save yourself, then do it now."

I knew I could never do that. So, I didn't pay any attention to what he said. I followed his voice. I left post-It notes for my trail, so I would know which way to get out of this damn place.

"Cassie, are you still in here?" This voice sounded like a teenager. And it sounded like she was right next to me. I saw a couple of holes. I stuck my arm through one. "Do you see my arm?" For an answer, she took my hand.

"Hang on." I talked to her as I looked around for a place where she could crawl to me. Even if she could crawl backward, I could help her back up.

"What's your name?"

"My name is Lucinda. My daddy calls me Linda."

"Are you ill, Lucinda?"

"No, my mom is the one who's ill. She was having her chemotherapy treatment. I don't know where I am right now. I was in the waiting room."

I looked around and backed up. I went a different way, and when I stuck my hand into the dark hole, I heard a gasp. "Lucinda, back up, honey." I kept hold of her foot as she did. When she was closer, I had to move a large chunk of cement. It was sharp, and I cut my hand on one of the sharp edges. But I didn't give a damn.

It took more moving of concrete, and then she was finally standing next to me, actually neither of us could stand up straight because it was impossible to stand straight. We were both crying.

"Do you have Lucinda?" Deanna asked.

"Yes, I'm taking her to where I saw the light. I'll be right back."

"Cassie, I agree with Doctor Ahmed. When you take Lucinda, you can go for help. And we can be saved."

I didn't say anything. There was no way I was going to leave one person down here. This building could shift at any time. I would be fighting for them to get out of here. As long as I could breathe, I would keep helping these people. My Post-It notes were life savers, but I stuck them where I couldn't get lost. They showed me where to go.

My body was starting to hurt, but I pushed myself. I had three people outside of this concrete cemetery already. I noticed the sun was going down, and I was starting to slow down. Doctor Ahmed stopped talking. I prayed he was still alive. I still had to find a way to Deanna. I promised to save her, and I would.

I decided to sit down for a quick rest. That's when I felt the rumble on the ground, and the concrete shifted. Not again. After only a small shake, it stopped. "Can everyone hear me?"

"Yes, I can hear you."

"I can hear you."

"Damn it, Cassie, get the hell out of here."

"About time you decided to talk. Did the shifting make it worse for you?"

"It's no change for me."

"No change for me either."

"Doctor Ahmed, what about you?"

"Nothing changed for me either."

"Can you all whisper so I can see who I'm closest to?" I followed. The voice sounded like a little boy who wasn't very far from me. I knew I would get him out before night, so I kept working. I had to turn around, I reached inside my pocket, and it was empty. *Where are my Post-It notes? Dammit. I have to find them.*

I returned to where I was, and there they were, along with the band-aids and the antiseptic cream. Damn, thirty minutes were wasted. I took a deep breath and tried to calm my nerves. I was starting to get scared that another earthquake was going to hit. I had to hurry.

I stuck my hands through all the holes I could see and felt around. I needed to see if there was a child in there. And then someone touched my fingers after I poked his belly. *There he is. How am I going to get him out?* I became frantic, looking for a way to get to the child. I was on my knees hunting. I was even looking to see if there was a way out that was low, but there wasn't anything. I would have to move pieces of concrete again.

I started feeling for all the loose concrete. The little pieces that I could lift. I couldn't lift all the heavy ones. I had to pull them out and let them fall. One hit me on my foot. *Damn it. That may have broken the little bones on the top of my foot. I'll keep my shoe on no matter what. I don't have a rap for my foot, so my shoe will have to do the trick. What am I going to do?* I moved one more big piece of concrete and I saw his leg.

"How did you get in here? Were you in here alone?" I asked as I rubbed his leg.

"No, my dad's in here somewhere. He told me to sit in that chair. That's where I was sitting. The chair is gone, I don't know where it is."

"Can you try and scoot backward?" He started scooting

backward and I felt sticky blood all over the side of his leg. *He must have a big gash there.* I pulled him out the rest of the way and hugged him. He could have been no more than nine years old.

"I have him," I said for the others to hear me. Everyone started laughing and crying at the same time. I held him until we came to a spot. I sat him on a concrete block and looked at his leg. I put some antiseptic on it, wrapped the gauze around it, and tied it into a knot. *That might help until he gets out and somebody can take care of it.*

"As soon as you get out, you go to where the ground is flat and stay away from all the concrete and the buildings. Now, promise me: I want you to tell whoever you see that we are down here. Can you do that for me?"

"Yes, I'll do it right away. I'll tell my dad. I know he's looking for me."

I prayed his father was alive. I noticed it was dark outside. "Are you okay about being in the dark?"

"Yes, I'm not scared of the dark."

"Good, I knew you were brave. I'll see you when I get out. You take care of yourself, okay?"

"You should try and get out now too." I didn't say anything, and then I kissed him on the forehead as I held him up so he could climb out.

I crawled back to where the others were. "It's dark outside right now. How about we start this back when the sun comes up?"

"That's a good idea," Deanna said. "I'm getting kind of tired myself."

"Deanna, can you move at all?"

"No. It's definitely a concrete casket that I'm in."

"If you can kick anything out with your feet, any little

bit, when I get to you, it'll be easier for me to get you out. Check to see if your arms can push anything."

"I thought you were going to sleep."

"I changed my mind. I'm coming for you, Deanna."

"One of my arms is under me. I can't move it, but I'll push whatever I can out of the way with the other one. I'm waiting for you, Cassie."

She's waiting for me. For some odd reason that made the tears fall from my eyes. *Luca, I need you.*

11

LUCA

I had a huge flashlight that one of the workers gave me. Where the hell could she be? I didn't even want to think about her underneath all that concrete. I looked over at Marlon, "Do you want to take a break? You haven't stopped since we got here."

"Neither have you. I will go as long as you do." He was as stubborn as his granddaughter.

"I hear someone crying," I said as I rushed to where the voice was. I walked around the building to see what that noise was. Four people were huddled together, crying. "What are you all doing here? Don't you know how dangerous it is? This ground keeps moving."

A teenage girl looked at me. "We don't want to leave here because we want to remember where the place is that we got out of, so that when she is finished helping everyone out, we'll know where to tell the people she is. We have to stay here. Look, there's another one."

I ran over and got the little boy off the pile of concrete. We looked at the child's leg and saw the white gauze on it.

My heart started beating fast. "How did you get out of there?" I asked the boy.

I felt I knew the answer already. Now I just needed them to tell me.

"Cassie helped me get out of there. She's gone back to help the other ones now. I told her to get out. She said she would see me in a little while. So, she's going to get out too. I want my daddy."

I looked at Marlon. He shook his head, "I am not surprised. How are we getting her out of there?"

The teenager spoke up. "She won't come out until everybody's out. Doctor Ahmed told her to get out, but she wouldn't. She told him she would leave when everyone left."

I ran to where the boy came from. I looked down at that small hole. "Cassie Rossi, you better get your butt out of there. Can you hear me, Cassie?"

"Luca. Luca, is that you? Where are you?"

"I'm where you just put the little boy through. I want you to return here, and I'll pull you out."

"Luca, I can't do that. I have to help the other ones. I have post-it notes all over my trail, and I won't get lost. I promise you I will be out in no time. First, I must help Deanna. She's waiting for me."

"I told her to get out. She's being too stubborn like she always is."

"That's doctor Ahmed," the girl said, looking between Marlon and me. "He told us Cassie was always stubborn, even before the earthquake."

"I need for you to run to where men are screaming for Cassie and tell them Luca wants them here. Can you do that for me?"

"Take this flashlight," Marlon said, handing his flashlight to the girl. "Cassie, you do what Luca says. Grab her the next time she gets close. We'll get her out of there."

"She's already gone. I can't go down there after her. I'm afraid the concrete will move if I try. Once we have all the guys here, we can figure it out. We'll have more light. I'm so glad we found her," I said, wiping my eyes. "I love her so much."

"I told you I knew that feeling. You only have that feeling once in a lifetime. Sometimes you'll get lucky and find the feeling again. I never found that feeling again. But I didn't go looking for it either."

"Here comes Dante and Serena."

"Where is she?" Dante demanded to know. He'd been a little crazy since he got here.

"She's down this hole. She won't leave until the others are out. She's helped these people out of there," I said, pointing to the group standing off to the side. "I told her to get out. She said she can't leave until everyone is out of there."

Dante went to the hole. "Cassie, can you hear me?"

"Daddy, is that you? Yes! Yes, I can hear you. It's like a big echo. Everyone can hear you down here."

"Good. I want you to get your butt back over here so we can get you out." Dante looked at me. "Did she just chuckle?"

I chuckled and took a deep breath. It felt so good to hear that laugh again. That meant our Cassie was okay. We were busy moving concrete and were so careful. We just wanted to get the big pieces out so everybody could get out. So far, she'd only gotten the younger people out.

I could hear her talking to someone. Someone named Deanna. I smiled to myself. She told Deanna she was coming for her. It was over an hour later that we heard them walking toward us. When they got to where I could see her, she looked up, and a huge smile was plastered on her face. She had so much cement dust on her I had to smile.

We reached down and pulled Deanna out. And before she knew what I would do, I also pulled Cassie out. I held her in my arms and kissed her face as she kissed me. All the while, she was trying to wiggle out to go back down the tunnel. "I missed you, sweetheart."

"Luca, I missed you so much. I still have people down there. I have to go back down; let me go."

"I'll go down there."

I saw the horrified look that came over her face. "There are places that you can't fit in. No, it would be best if you didn't get hurt. Just let me go. I know the way. I've got all the post-it notes everywhere telling me where to go. Let me come with you."

"No, go to your mom and your grandfather. Kiss me for luck."

"I'll go with him," her father said after he hugged her. We saw the frightened look come into her eyes again.

"Hey, where do you think you got your bravery from?"

She slowly nodded, turned, and went to where her mom and grandpa stood. I watched when she saw the young ones that she had rescued. She started crying, as she ran to them.

"We should see if we can find your family. How come you guys are waiting here? I told you to find your parents."

"We didn't want to leave you here. We were scared to go. We had to make sure we remembered where you were. In case there was another earthquake."

"Thank you," Cassie said, hugging the teenager. She kissed her on the cheek.

"Does anybody have a phone for Deanna to call her husband?"

Her grandfather hugged her and handed his phone over to Deanna. We heard a man cry out as he ran to the boy. He picked him up and held him in his arms. "This is Cassie. She helped us out of there."

"Thank you so much."

"You're welcome."

~

"Damn, it's tight down here," Dante said, walking slowly behind me. "I don't know how she did this without a flashlight. I can't see two inches in front of me."

"She did it by voice. She would have them whispering so she would know who she was close to."

"I take it you are, Doctor Ahmed?"

"Yes. I don't think you can get to me. I tried telling Cassie that, but she's so stubborn."

"Why do you think we can't get you out?" I asked as I listened to where his voice was.

"Because I'm stuck between some concrete pieces, and one is in my back. Hopefully, it's not too far in my back."

"Dante, we need to move some of these big chunks. But when we do, we have to have a place to put them, so it won't block our exit."

"I agree with you. I want whoever is left down here whispering. Tell me where you're at so we won't put any concrete in the path to get you out of here."

I heard four voices, not counting Doctor Ahmed's. I wasn't leaving him behind. "Doctor Ahmed, where are you at?" It took a while before he answered me.

"I'm right here."

I felt like if I turned my head, I would see him. Then I realized there was a big concrete wall between us. I looked every which way to see how I could get to him. Then I looked up. I would have to climb over the concrete wall. I looked at Dante, and he shook his head. I knew he thought it was too dangerous. I wondered how Cassie figured she would get him out. I'd have to ask her when I see her.

I pulled myself up on top of a chunk of cement and then another. I looked down, and I could see Doctor Ahmed. I took the flashlight and shined it down to where he was. He moved his head back and looked up at me. "I'm going to get you out of here." I knew I could reach him. He was tall, so all he would have to do was raise his arms for us to grab.

"That's what Cassie said. But I have to tell you guys, if you try to move me, I'm afraid the building will be moved more, and you will be stuck here with me. And then you know Cassie will risk her life in a more dangerous place. I don't want you stuck in this concrete casket with me."

I ignored what he was saying. I was trying to find out which piece of concrete I could move to get him out of there. I saw the one pushed against his back. He cried out when I tested it with my foot to see if we could get away from his back.

"Does that cause you a lot of pain? Can you move your arms at all?

"I can move one of them."

"Reach back and see if you can feel how much of that piece of concrete is in your back."

"There's a lot of concrete pushed against my back. I don't believe it has damaged any organs. My back may be fractured but it's not on my spine because I can still move my feet and hands."

"I'm going to push it back away from you. Dante will pull you up. It will hurt, but we'll have you out of there in no time." I looked down at Dante, and he hopped up next to me. "Dante, I will push this back and you grab his arm to pull him up."

It took us probably thirty minutes before we were able to get him up. There would have been no way Cassie could get him out of there, and I knew she would have been torn into a million pieces about what to do. Dante put him over his shoulder and carried him out while I went to help the next person.

"I think we have everyone," Dante said as the sun was coming up.

I pulled myself halfway out of the hole and saw Cassie counting. I knew we had missed someone. But I didn't know where that person would be because no one answered when I called.

"I don't see the little girl," she said as big tears started to fall from her eyes. I knew she was so tired. She wouldn't stop until everyone was out. "I know where she is. I'm going to get her out of there."

"Damn it, Cassie. I will find her. I'm not letting you go back into that concrete grave."

"Do you think I could live a happy life if I didn't bring that little girl out of there? I have to do this. You can carry her when I find her, but I will get her out of there."

"We'll get her together, and then we are going home. And you aren't going to go anywhere for a while."

"Thank you," she said as she kissed me and lowered herself into the hole. I wrapped my arms around her. "I love you, sweetheart, so you be careful."

"I will be. You be careful too. Now, let's go get that little girl."

It took a while for Cassie to remember exactly where she heard the girl's voice coming from. When she did remember, I frowned. "I don't think you can get in there." There was no way in hell I was letting her squeeze her body between those concrete blocks. One little shake, and she would be gone. "You'll get stuck if you go in there."

"No, I won't. I've done it before. How do you think I got the other little ones out? I had to squeeze my body through and pull them out. Help me up there."

I did nothing at first. I could only picture her in that very little spot and the concrete falling on her body. I knew she was staring at me, so I didn't look at her. My back was blocking the entrance of that damn little hole. I was trying to think. I couldn't decide what to do, and Cassie was impatient. I felt it by the way her foot was tapping. Then I opened my eyes and looked at her. "Okay, but this better be quick."

"It will be. Help me up." I watched her crawl into that tight space that was tighter than anything. Her hips squeezed through that skinny spot. She had to keep her arms over her head to press her body through. I couldn't breathe as I watched her, knowing how dangerous this was.

"I have her. I'm going to pull her back. She's unconscious right now, but I feel a pulse. We have her. That's all that counts." I watched as she backed up, pulling a little girl. I got her ankles and dragged her to me when she was within my reach. That's when I noticed she only had one shoe on.

"Let me have her." I looked at the little girl, who was no more than four or five. I kissed my woman. "You are the bravest person I know. You saved all these people. Let's get this little one to her family." I hoped her parents were alive.

12

CASSIE

We had been at my grandpa's place for a week, but it was time to go home. "I wish you lived where we lived."

"You know, I wish the same thing, sweetie," Grandpa said, hugging me.

My mom hugged me, "I will miss you so much. We'll see you next week. We're going to visit with the baby. We're going to visit with all of you, not only the baby." We giggled together. Sometimes it seems like I've always known my mom. It doesn't seem like we grew up without our mom and dad. When my uncles kidnapped Sara and me, we were babies. We found our family last year and so much has changed for our family since we found them.

Luca was acting strange, "What is wrong with you?"

"Why do you think something is wrong?"

"Because you have walked around me six times."

"I'm sorry. I was just wondering if you..."

"What?"

"Cassie, I love you so much. I will love you until the day I die. I know you are my one and only…" He took a deep breath and looked around.

My family had moved in close, waiting for something. Luca swallowed and licked his lips. Then he ran his hand through his hair. "Cassie, will you marry me?"

"Yes," my grandpa said. My mom and dad burst into laughter.

I smiled at Luca and shook my head. "Yes, Luca, I will marry you. Are you sure you want to marry me?"

"Yes, he's sure," Grandpa said.

Luca pulled me to him and kissed me. Then we were showered in hugs and kisses. Tears fell from my eyes as I looked at my mom and dad. "I'm so happy both of you will be at my wedding. Daddy can walk me down the aisle. Mama, you can help me plan our wedding."

"It will be short planning because we are getting married when they come to visit the baby. That will give you two weeks."

"Okay, we can do that," my mom said.

"I'm so happy for you two," Grandpa said, hugging us. I saw him kiss Luca on the cheek and wipe his eyes. "You have made me very happy today. I'll see you in two days."

"Grandpa, I can't wait for you to visit us." I looked at Luca, "Am I going to live with you?"

"Yes, darling, you will be living with me. Starting when we get home."

"That is such a relief," my dad said, then he hurried and hugged me. I chuckled because I knew he was relieved that I would have Luca to keep an eye on me.

"We'll see all of you soon." I hugged my little sister, Alyssa, "I want you to be the flower girl at my wedding. Would you like that?"

"Yes, that will be so fun. Do I get to throw rose petals when it's my turn?"

"Yes, we'll make sure we have lots of rose petals."

"I love all of you," I said as we entered the airport. Everyone came with us to the airport to say goodbye.

We were seated on the plane when a woman stopped and looked at Luca. "Luca, it's been a long time."

"Cheryl, how have you been?"

"I've been good. What about you?"

"I'm doing great. Let me introduce you to my fiancée, Cassie." Luca looked at me, and I smiled. "Cassie, this is Cheryl, an old friend."

Cheryl arched her perfect eyebrow. "We were almost family at one time. If you hadn't gone to prison, you would have married my sister."

"Lucky for me, you went to prison," I said, then I chuckled at the look on Luca's face.

Luca chuckled. "Lucky for you and me that you date ex-felons," he said, quickly kissing my lips. His eyes softened as he gazed into my eyes. I think he forgot Cheryl stood looking at us.

"It was nice meeting you, Cheryl," I said, smiling at her.

"Yes, it was nice meeting you."

"Are you headed back home?" Luca asked. I could tell he was ready for her to walk away.

"Yes, we are headed home. I wasn't going to say anything. I don't know how to tell you this, so I'll just say it. You have a son. He's sitting up front. I'm surprised Donna hasn't told you about him."

"Are you telling me I have a nine-year-old son?"

"That's what I said. I would never have told you, except I heard you lied about killing that man. Jenna killed him because of what he did to her. He deserved to die. What I'm saying is if you were still in prison, I would have never told you about your son. I have no idea why Donna didn't call you. But I think it would be great for your son to know his father. He needs his dad to teach him boy stuff. Of course, my sister might think differently."

"I want a DNA test, and after that, I'll talk to Donna about what is going to happen."

My heart was pounding, so I knew Luca's must have been. I heard the shift in his breathing. "What is his name?" I asked Cheryl.

"His name is Michael."

"Does he have my last name," Luca asked. I knew he was angry. He had a tic in his jawline. I reached over and took his hand. He wrapped his fingers around mine.

"Yes, he has your last name."

"I'll see Donna at the hospital at three tomorrow," Luca said, finishing the conversation.

"As you wish, I'll inform Donna." She walked away.

Neither of us said a word for a while. Finally, I couldn't stay quiet a moment longer. "That was surprising. Do you want me to run and get a photo of Michael for you?"

"How will you do that?" he whispered.

"With my phone."

"I know, but don't you think that might scare him?"

"He'll never know I'm around."

"Okay, but be careful. I don't want you to get in trouble."

"Hey, I'll be like a ghost. They'll never know I'm there." I kissed him before getting up. I made my way to where Cheryl had gone. I stood in the flight attendant's spot. At first, all I could do was watch him as he played with the phone. I knew when Cheryl spotted me, she said something to Michael, and he raised his head so I could get a clear photo of his face.

He was beautiful, and he looked just like his daddy. He was big for nine, also like his daddy. I wondered what color eyes he had. I would bet anything they were a stormy gray. I took about twenty photos of him before I got up and returned to where Luca sat waiting for me.

I sat down and wiped a tear from my eye. I turned to him and said, "He looks just like his daddy." Luca bent his head. I knew he wanted to cry, but we were on an airplane surrounded by people. "I'll transfer all the photos to your phone. That way, you can look at them whenever you want. He's beautiful."

13

LUCA

I couldn't quit staring at the photos. He looked just like me. He had my hair. He had my smile. He even had dimples on his cheeks. I wanted to pick him up and hold him in my arms. This was my son. I knew it. I'd been out of prison for four years. Donna had four years to tell me that I had a son. I looked at my phone, and then I called Mace.

I got his voicemail. "Hey, Mace, I need you. Can you call me back? Thanks. Bye."

"What are you going to do?" Cassie asked.

"I'm going to fight for my parental rights. This is my son, and I will fight for him."

"Good, I think that's what you should do."

I was quiet for the rest of the ride home. All I could think about was my son sitting on a plane with me, and I couldn't even go over and say, 'Hello, Michael, I'm your dad.' As soon as I got Mace to help me with this, I would establish my parental rights and have as many rights as his mother. I'd be able to take Michael with me, to do things with him. I wondered what his middle name was. He was using my last name, so she couldn't claim she didn't know he was mine.

"How do you feel right now?" Cassie asked me, holding my hand.

"I don't know how I feel. I feel afraid. What if he doesn't like me? What if he hates me because I never knew him? What if he doesn't want to get to know me?"

"He's going to love you. What little boy wouldn't want a father just like you? You are kind, you are strong, and you are a hero. He's going to love you. He's nine years old. Look at Sarah and me. We just found out about my parents last year and they love us, and we love them. You're going to have a wonderful life with your son."

"Thank you. I can't wait to meet him." I ran my hand through my hair and down my face. "I want to hear his voice. I want to hear him laugh. I'm going to hold him in my arms. He's my son. How could she keep him away from me?"

"Who broke off the engagement?"

"Donna broke up with me. To be truthful, I was glad she did. I didn't feel like I loved her enough to marry her. Not like I love you. I'll love you forever. I stopped loving her after a few months of being in prison. So that proves I didn't love her. I should never have allowed her to talk us into becoming engaged."

"I'll have the wife I want. I'll have my son, and we'll have lots more kids."

"How many more kids?"

"Five, maybe?"

"Let's make it three more kids."

"Okay, three more kids. Let's talk about our wedding. Where do you want to go on our honeymoon?"

"I want to stay home on my honeymoon. I haven't been

home in a long time. Somewhere safe, warm, and cozy. That's all I want. Tell me about your house."

"It's our house. It's a big Victorian. It belonged to my grandma's family. Grandma left it to me when she passed away. I've been working on it, fixing it up, and modernizing it. I've added two more bathrooms. I think you are going to love it."

"I already do love it. It doesn't matter where I live. All I want is someplace that I can call home. Sara and I were always moving with my parents. Well, I know now that they weren't my parents. Our uncles kidnapped us when we were babies. One uncle took me, and the other took Sara. Sara moved in with us when she was seven."

We talked about everything. She really did try to take my mind off things. Cassie eventually went to sleep. I would have, but I could not get Michael off my mind. I wondered if Donna had said anything to him about me. Did he know I was his father? Was he going to be happy when I came into his life?

We landed at our first stopover. Luckily for me, they allowed some of us to deplane from the back and others from the front. I came down the stairs of the plane and walked towards the terminal. I waited with Cassie. We stood at the floor-to-ceiling window looking out at the tarmac as I hoped I hadn't missed them. I hadn't. Cheryl came towards the terminal with Michael holding onto her hand. He was laughing at something; he must have thought it was funny. I even chuckled just seeing him laugh. I looked at Cassie, and she was smiling.

"He's a happy kid," I said as we turned away from the window and rushed up the escalator. I didn't want him to see me.

"Yes, he is," Cassie said, with sadness in her voice.

"Why are you sad?"

"I'm not sad. I just had a sad moment thinking about Michael. I remember when Sara thought her parents were dead. When she thought her family had been murdered, she was seven. She had a sense of sadness for the longest time. Michael will know his father. I'm happy about that. We didn't know our parents. It took twenty-eight years for us to know who our parents were. I'm sad about that."

I wrapped my arms around her. "You'll be a wonderful mom."

"I know I will, and you will be a wonderful father. I have never asked you why you went to prison for six years. Do you want to tell me now?"

"My sister, Jenna, has a mental disability. This man abused her we thought was our friend. He brutally raped Jenna, and she killed him. I knew she could never be locked up, so I said I killed him for what he did to Jenna. I was there for six years when I found out my sisters needed me. Opal helped get me out. She's a lawyer, who I met when I lived in Maine. She married Nick Lombardi. He's an ex-Army Ranger."

"Your poor sister. I can't stand to think of you in prison. How are your sisters doing?"

"They're doing good now. I'll invite them to the wedding."

"You better. I want to meet all of your family. Maybe they can come for a visit."

"My main thought right now is to get everything straightened out about my son. That's all I'm thinking of right now."

"I understand. Of course, that's what is the most important thing right now. Do Donna and Michael live in Oregon?"

"No, they live in Maine. I'm sure she hasn't left there. She has so many friends, and I'm sure she wouldn't move away from them or her family."

"That is so far away."

"I know it is." My phone rang, and I answered. "Hello?"

"Hey, what's up?"

"I was on an airplane, and I ran into Cheryl. Do you remember her? Donna's sister."

"How was that?"

"Well, not like I'd expect it to be. Cheryl said I have a son. So, Cassie took some pictures of him. He looks just like me. He's big for nine, just like I was my entire life. He has my eyes and my dimples. I want my son," I growled. Cassie looked at me. "Sorry."

"Did you meet him?"

"No, I'm going to get a DNA tomorrow. I'm supposed to meet her at the hospital in Maine at three and get it on paper that Michael is mine. He has my last name."

"That's good on your side."

"I don't want to take him from his mother. You know Donna, I'm sure she's a great mom. I want some rights. I wish we lived in the same town. It would make it so much easier."

"Do you think you might move to Maine?"

"I don't know. My sisters still live there but I am building a life here. I am getting married to Cassie in two weeks." I didn't want Cassie to feel left out, so I put my arm around her. Then it dawned on me that I would have to talk to Cassie about whatever I decided. We were going to be married. Did I forget I wasn't doing this alone? I'd talk to her.

"I'll draw up some papers for you to get started. Are you going straight to Maine or coming by here?"

"I'll be in Oregon in a couple of hours."

"Are they still on the same plane as you?"

"No, they took the flight to Maine."

"Okay, I'll see you when you get here."

"Thanks, Mace." I turned and looked at Cassie, "You know I would never make any decision without discussing it with you, right?"

"Yes, I know that. You do what you need to do, though. I understand. Don't worry that you will hurt my feelings if you forget to tell me something. Go to Maine and take care of your son."

"Do you want to go with me?"

"No. I have a wedding to plan."

"As long as you know how much I love you. I will always love you. Even after we are not on this planet, I will still love you."

"I know. I love you too."

"I didn't mean to ignore you."

"Luca, stop worrying. You didn't ignore me. I'm a big girl. I'm thirty. I'm not offended at all."

"Good." I bent my head and kissed her. "Are you going to be staying at our house?"

"I will move in when we are married."

"I thought we decided you would move in today."

"You're going to be busy, and so am I."

"Okay, but you go home with me on our wedding day."

"I can't wait for that day."

14

CASSIE

"Sara, she is so perfect. I don't want to put her down."

"I'm the same way. Eventually, I make myself put her down but then Ethan picks her up. If it's not us, then it's Ethan's brother, Scott. He is such a good baby."

"He is indeed. I'm so happy for you. Oh, I forgot to tell you that Grandpa will be here in a few days. And Mama is going to help me plan a quick wedding."

She started jumping and screaming, I had to shush her. I was happy that my parents didn't tell her before I could. "I am so happy for you. Let me see the ring," she took my hand and gawked at the ring. "Where is the groom?"

"That's what I wanted to talk to you about. We were on the airplane coming home when this woman approached Luca. It turns out she was his ex-fiancée's sister. She told him that he had a nine-year-old son. Of course, Luca said he wanted a blood test. That's where he is. He went to Maine. He's meeting her at the hospital tomorrow. But that little boy looks just like him. Look at the photos I took on the airplane."

"He was on the same airplane as you?"

"Yes. That's his aunt. Her name is Cheryl."

"She looks nice. Why did they break up?"

"Well, Luca went to prison; he got life in prison. But then the truth came out after six years. She didn't want her son to know his father was in prison for murder."

"Yeah, that's right. I was told that his sister killed a man who brutally raped her, and Luca said he did it. Until his sisters needed him, and then the truth came out. Does he plan on moving back to Maine?"

"I don't know. I don't think Luca even knows yet. It's too soon to know what will happen."

"But you believe this is his child?"

"Yes, Michael is his son. He has Luca's dimples and looks just like him. I feel Luca will want to live in Maine, where his son lives. He said he would discuss everything with me before he did anything. I suggested we postpone the wedding for a few months, but Luca doesn't want to. I know he loves me."

Sara was holding the baby now. I pulled my hair back and started braiding it, which was a habit I had when I was nervous. "His son has to come first. You and I know that. I think we should put the wedding off for a while. Luca didn't know about his son until he'd already picked a date for the wedding."

"I think you are right. Talk to Luca tonight. Tell him you'll get married in two months. That gives him time to be with his son."

"I'll call him this evening. He wanted me to move into his house, but I told him I would move in after we were married."

"Are you sad?"

"A little. I feel like I'm walking a tightrope and don't know if I will fall. What if he wants to get back with Donna because he wants to be with his son all the time?"

"That's not going to happen. That man loves you; nothing will make him give you up."

"I hope so. Okay, I think I'll go lie down for a while."

"Okay, I'm going to put the baby to bed. He's sleeping."

I couldn't relax, so I put my running clothes on. I decided to run on the beach. The one thing I could do was run. When I first started running, I couldn't understand how it was a workout in self-defense, but now I know it's the main part of your workout. I love running. My mind can get clear, and I can plan my wedding.

I ran about ten miles one way before I turned around to head back. "Do you need some water? You haven't stopped to rest."

I looked over and smiled. "My legs burn if I stop for any length of time." I looked at the beautiful woman as she passed me a water bottle.

"My name is Gabby. I'm Ryker's wife. This is our home."

I paused, jogging in place. "Hi, Gabby. Your house is beautiful. My name is Cassie Rossi. I love your music. I'm sorry I can't stay and visit, I have ten miles still to go."

"Why do you run so far?"

"Sometimes I forget I'm running. We are getting married within the next few weeks, and you two have to be there," I called out as Ryker approached us.

Gabby smiled. "Who are you marrying?"

Ryker called out to her. "I told you Luca was getting married. Cassie is who we went to get from India."

Gabby smiled. "Ohhhhh." Ryker was standing next to his wife now. "That's Luca's house right there," she said, pointing. "So, I guess you'll live there, and we'll be neighbors." All three of us were suddenly visibly frightened by a scream. Gabby and Ryker looked back and ran toward their house, and I followed. When we got inside, there were two children, a boy and a girl. The little girl was turning blue. The little boy looked frightened. He was obviously the one who screamed.

Gabby picked up the child. She was trembling. Ryker took her from a distraught Gabby. "What's wrong with her?" Gabby cried.

"Give her to me," I said, holding out my arms.

"I think she's choking," Ryker said.

I took the child from him and worked to get something from her throat. I tipped her head back and looked around.

"What do you need?"

Something flat that can stick into her throat. Gabby was panicking. She handed me a file. I pushed the child's tongue down, and I saw it. Something was lodged there, but I couldn't get it out, so I pushed it down. The little girl wasn't breathing, so I gave her mouth-to-mouth until she took a breath. I handed the screaming child to her parents, who were crying as loud as the child. "Take her to the hospital, get an x-ray, and tell them she needs to stay all night so they can keep an eye on her."

"How can I ever repay you?" Gabby asked.

"You just did. Now go, get to the hospital quickly."

"Can you please stay with Mathew until my mom gets here?" Ryker asked.

"Yes, now go. One other thing. Walk into where the ambulance enters, not the main entrance." The little boy was still crying when they left. "Let's have ice cream," I said as I picked him up. He told me where the ice cream was. We were outside playing for a while. When I looked up, Luca stood there watching me. Mathew ran to Luca, and he picked him up.

"Sweetheart, what are you doing here?"

"I'm eating ice cream with Mathew until his grandmother gets here. I thought you were on a plane somewhere." I walked to him, and he pulled me into his arms and kissed me. He held both Mathew and me in his arms.

"Ewwwww," Mathew complained, burying his face into Luca's neck.

Luca tickled him. "I decided I wanted to stay with you tonight. I can go to Maine tomorrow. Now, tell me what happened."

I told him about the little girl. "I'm so glad I ran today and was here when this happened."

"Damn, I wonder what she choked on."

"I think it was a marble. That's why I told them to have her x-rayed.

That's when the grandmother drove up. She was upset about her granddaughter. "She's going to be fine," I said as she walked into the backyard. "Her throat might be sore, but she will be fine. That's what is important. Maybe this will keep her from putting things in her mouth."

"Millicent is a terror. Her father has spoiled her rotten. She runs to him for everything. I'm sorry dear, what is your name?"

"Rose, this is my fiancée, Cassie Rossi. We are getting married in two weeks, so you must attend our wedding. We'll call you as soon as we figure out all the details."

"Cassie, it is a pleasure meeting you. Ryker told us how brave you were in getting those people out of the collapsed hospital in India."

"Thank you, I'm happy to know you too, Rose. I'm sure we will be great friends."

"Yes, we will. I have to run now, I wish I had turned my stove off, but I have a stew cooking on it. When Ryker called me, I took off, not even thinking about what was cooking."

15

LUCA

I looked over at Cassie and laughed. "It's a miracle that you ran past Ryker's home when Millie was choking."

"Yes, and Gabby was the one who stopped me and offered me a bottle of water. I was so surprised when she said you lived in this home. You live on the beach. I love this place. Did you plant all of these flowers?"

"No, my great granny and my grandma planted the flowers. Now you can put your own touch in the garden also. Gabby always has a vegetable garden and will give you tons of veggies."

"I love fresh veggies. Now, walk me through my new home."

I admit, I was a little nervous showing Cassie through our house. The home that she would have forever. The home that we would raise our children in. I prayed she loved it as much as I did. She didn't say anything as she walked from room to room. I knew it needed a woman's touch, and she would make it a home we would love.

Finally, I couldn't stand the silence for a moment any longer. "Well, could you live in this home and raise our family?" For answers, she started crying. I wrapped my arms around her. "Why are you crying?"

"Because I love this house. I've always dreamed of a home just like this to live in with my family. I will be proud to live in this house where your relatives lived. I will be proud to plant some flowers like your grandma and great-grandma did. I never thought I would ever live in the house that was in my dreams. And here it is. I'll live here with the man I love for the rest of my life. Thank you for choosing me to be your wife. I love you so much."

"I love you too, sweetheart. I can't wait for us to get married. Please come with me tomorrow?"

"Are you sure you want me there with you?"

"I need you to be with me. You're my strength. I know I'm going to need all the strength I have to face my son."

"Yes, I'll go with you. Your son is going to love you. There's no reason for you to be nervous."

"We can pick out his bedroom and then fix it as a boy's room. He can help us. He's lucky to have you for his dad. I know you're going to be the best father. Look how little Matthew ran to you. I fed him ice cream, but he still wanted you. He didn't want his ice cream; he only wanted you."

"Now, are you going to show me our room?"

"Yes, now I will." I took her hand and walked her to the master bedroom. It was one of the rooms I had already remodeled. "I put all-natural paint tones here because I didn't know what I wanted yet. The bed is brand new. Do you like it?"

"Oh, Luca, I love it. I love everything about this room. The master bathroom is so beautiful. That beautiful bath-tub, it's like you remodeled it just for me."

"I'll let you pick out the linen. I thought we could get a

couple of chairs, put them in here, and read to our children."

"We'll have a wonderful life together, you and me, and our children. I automatically mean Michael in saying our children. To me, Michael is our child. And I don't like the word stepmom. I just like the word mom. He will be happy when he's with us because we are happy. Your children act how you act. If you are miserable, then they will be miserable. If you are happy, then they will be happy... I should call Sara and tell her where I am."

"Okay, you call Sara while I undress you."

Cassie slept in my arms, in our huge new bed. I wanted to ensure it would be large enough for our children to climb in with us so we could read stories or just hold them close. I was anxious to meet Michael. Finally, my eyes drifted shut.

∽

WE LEFT Oregon and headed to Maine. My stomach ached. I hadn't been this nervous in my entire life. I just wanted my son to love me, as I already loved him. Cassie reached over and took my hand in hers, which worked wonders. I picked our hands up and kissed hers.

We were at the hospital getting tested when Cheryl showed up with Michael. "Michael, sweetie, this is your daddy." She looked at me, "I talked to the lab, and they said you are his father. I need to talk to you about Donna. She isn't well. She has cancer. I've been taking care of Michael most of the time. I love him more than anything, but he needs his daddy. Donna needs help. It's depressing for a child to be with her constantly. He needs you."

I hadn't taken my eyes off my son. "Hello, Michael. I

would have been with you if I had known I had a son. I'm so happy to be your father. Are you happy?"

"Wait, you're my dad?"

"Yes. Does that bother you?"

"No, I've been waiting to find you. Mom told me all about you. She wanted to have me with her a little longer because she would miss me. That's why she never told you about me. Don't be mad at Mom."

"I'm not mad at her. I'm happy I have you."

"I will miss my mom. She is a good mom, and I love her."

I picked him up and held him in my arms. He wrapped his arms around me, and I prayed my tears didn't fall because I didn't want my son to see me cry. I looked at Cassie, and she had tears falling from her eyes.

"Are you going to be hugging me a lot?"

"Probably. Does it bother you if I hug you"

"No, Mom and Aunt Cheryl always hug me. I didn't know if dads hugged all the time."

"This dad will be giving you lots of hugs."

"Okay. Who is that?" he asked, looking at Cassie.

I looked at her. She was busy wiping her eyes and blowing her nose. "This is Cassie. We are getting married in a couple of weeks. I would love for you to be at our wedding."

"Does she like kids?"

I heard Cassie chuckle. "I love kids. Now I would like to meet your mom."

"Would you?" I asked, looking at the love of my life.

"Yes, let's go."

Cheryl was also blowing her nose and wiping her eyes. "We'll follow you," Cassie said.

"Okay."

"Cheryl, where do you live?" Cassie asked.

"I've been staying here lately, but I live in London. I have a design business."

"What do you design?" Cassie wanted to know.

"Women's clothes."

"I bet you're popular."

"I'm getting there. It's a lot of work, but it's the kind of work that I love doing."

"You're a great sister and a wonderful aunt. I'm happy I will be related to you."

"But you will only be related to Michael."

"You're Michael's family, so that makes you our family."

Cheryl started crying. "I was so worried about who would be taking care of Michael. It is such a relief knowing he will be showered with love. I am honored to be your sister, Cassie."

"Give me your keys, and I'll drive you. We'll come back tonight for the rental," I said. Damn, I was the luckiest man on earth. I wanted to take Cassie in my arms, kiss and hold her. She was more giving than anyone I knew. I couldn't help myself. I took Cassie by her shoulders and kissed her. I heard Michael giggle and Cheryl chuckle. Cassie got into the backseat with Michael.

"What grade are you in, Michael?"

"I will be in the fourth when school starts back. Do they have a good school where my dad lives?"

"Yes, they have a great school there. You're going to love it. Tell me what you like to do."

"I like to play video games. I have an Xbox. I know how to play baseball and football. I'm really smart. That's what my mom says."

"I'm sure she's right. I've never played games. It sounds like fun."

"It is a lot of fun."

Cassie talked to him all the way home. I still needed to speak to Donna about visiting rights. It didn't dawn on me that she was as sick as she was. When I walked inside her house, she was sleeping on the recliner. Michael put his fingers to his lips. "Mom is sleeping. We have to let her rest."

"Of course, we do."

"Michael, finish packing," Cheryl said. We followed her into the kitchen. Cheryl made some coffee while we sat at the table.

"How long has she been this sick?"

"A couple of months. Donna was diagnosed five years ago. She didn't know what to do because you were in prison. She came to visit you, but they wouldn't let her in so she could talk to you. She wrote you like ten letters. Donna never thought you killed anyone. She thought it went as it did, but you picked prison instead of her."

"I never received a letter from her. I would have told the truth and gotten out of prison."

"We thought the cancer was gone, but it came back. The doctor says she has maybe six months to live. I didn't know what else to do. When I saw you, it was like fate. It really was fate. I was going to call you when I got back home. I was so happy to see that you are marrying someone like Cassie. I liked her from the beginning."

"Who takes care of Donna?" Cassie asked.

"I've been caring for her. If I have to go out of town like I was in Italy, I hire someone to stay with her and take Michael with me. I just don't want strangers to take care of my sister. But I'm about to lose my business because I haven't paid attention to my work. I haven't been able to do any designs. I can't concentrate on my work while I'm here. This sounds selfish, but I can't do designs beautiful gowns while my sister is lying in bed dying."

Cassie nodded. "Of course, you haven't had any time to work." Then she turned toward me, "Let's take Donna home with us." She could have knocked me over with a feather. I was so surprised when that came out of her mouth. "I can take care of her; I'll get help. She can be with her son, and Michael can be with his mom. It's unfair that she must be alone without her child."

Cheryl looked at me like Cassie was crazy. And then she started crying again. I got up from the table. I walked over to Cassie, picked her up, and hugged her. What other woman would be this unselfish to want to take care of my son's mother?

"Are you going to say something?" she asked.

"I'm trying to think what I should say. I know that would be the best thing for Michael, but what about you? Do you realize how hard this will be?"

"Yes, I know how hard it will be. That's why we will get help. But we'll know who is helping her. It won't be a stranger. This is what your son and Donna need. Cheryl has to start working again, or she will lose her business. That's a tough position that she's in right now. Do you want to see her lose her business?" I didn't say anything. "We'll Charter a plane and take Donna home with us. When Cheryl wants to visit with us, all she has to do is come there. She's more than welcome. The house is big. It can hold all of us."

"Okay. I'll Charter a plane." I looked at Cheryl who was still crying. "Do you want to pack some things? What about this house? Who's going to pack it up?"

"I'll take care of all of that. She's renting this house, so it's not hers. We don't have to sell anything. I'll pack all her stuff up and what I think she wants to give to Michael, I'll ship to your house. Cassie, do you know what you're doing? You are the most wonderful woman I've ever met. Michael's going to be so happy."

"Why am I going to be happy?"

"Michael, your dad is taking your mom home with you guys, and Cassie will take care of her."

"Cassie is going to take care of my mom?" I watched as my son walked over to Cassie. He gave her the biggest hug, and then he broke down crying. Cassie pulled him onto her lap. And both of them hugged each other.

"That means I don't have to visit with Mom. Now I can just stay with her all the time while she's sick. Mom is going to be so happy. I'm so happy. Thank you, Cassie."

"I'll do anything for you, sweetheart."

And I knew she would. Because Cassie already thought of Michael as her child. "How about if we take care of everything? We'll see you here tomorrow morning. You can explain to Donna what we're going to do. I suppose we should ask her first if that's what she wants."

"I never thought about asking her," Cassie said. "What is wrong with me? Of course, we must ask Donna if she wants to go home with us."

"Do I hear my sweet boy in the kitchen?" Michael ran out of the kitchen and into the living room where his mom was. We followed behind him. "Luca," she gasped, looking at me. She started sobbing. "I'm so glad you're here... I was so scared about what to do with Michael. Things are bad, Luca. I don't have long." She paused and sobbed even more. "You will have to take him with you."

"We're taking both of you."

"I don't understand what you mean," she said, wiping at her cheek.

"Donna, you're going home with us too." She looked

from me to Cassie, then back to me. "Are you guys crazy? Why would you want to take me with you?"

"So I can be with you longer, Mom. Please say yes. Please say yes."

Donna looked at Cassie. "You must be the crazy one."

"I've been called that a time or two," she shrugged. "Hi Donna, I'm Cassie. I love Michael already. I want you to not worry about anything anymore. I'm a registered nurse. I'm going to take care of you."

"You mean you really want to do this?" She looked at Cheryl, who was crying again. "Cheryl, what should I do?"

"You want to spend more time with your son, and you will have someone like Cassie taking care of you. She said she would get help, too, so you won't have to worry about it only being her. I think this is perfect. I feel like God has sent her to us. You know, my business was going downhill. I was running low on money."

"I know." She looked at Cassie. "I don't want to mess up your relationship with Luca. Have you guys talked this over?"

"Yes, Luca agrees with me. Michael wants his mommy around him longer than a little while. That will give him and you more time together. You can sit in a lounger and watch the ocean while Luca plays ball with his son on the beach."

She looked between us then at Michael. A smiled graced her lips as she looked back at Cassie, "Yes, I would love that. I can spend more time with Michael."

"And I can spend more time with you," Michael said as he crawled up next to his mama.

16

CASSIE

I still could not believe the beautiful wedding dress I received today from an overnight courier from France. I opened the box and almost fell to my knees. It was the most beautiful wedding dress I have ever seen, and it was mine. Cheryl made this dress for me. I called her right away and thanked her a million times.

Then it dawned on me and that was replaced by worry. I never thought my mom would have a wedding dress made for me until the dress showed up at my home with a beautiful note from my mom a few days ago. It worried me like crazy until my sister entered our house carrying the baby.

"He is so beautiful. I remember when Michael was a baby," Donna said, smiling. I hurried and ran and got my tablet. Whenever Donna told a story about Michael as a baby, I wrote everything down. So, when he asked if he was like that when he was little, I could say yes or no. I also taped Donna talking to Michael about things she wanted to tell him when he got older. Something that reminded him how much his mama loved him. It broke my heart to know she was dying.

"Sara, Mama sent me a dress, and I have the most wonderful idea." Sara looked at me like I was crazy and didn't want to hear what I had to say. I don't know why she thought it would be something bad. "It's nothing bad. It's a wonderful idea. Since you got married on a plane or wherever it was, I thought we could have a double wedding, and Daddy could walk us both down the aisle."

"Cassie, I don't want to take away from your special day. No, this is your time."

"I wasn't thinking about myself. I was thinking about Mama. She had this beautiful dress made, and no one to wear it because I'm wearing the one Cheryl made for me. But if you and Ethan get married with the family around, and we can all share your wedding, Mama's feelings won't be hurt when I don't wear her dress."

"Let me see it."

"I'll get it." I ran to my room and got the dress. As I walked back in, Donna held Baby Dante in her arms. I smiled, knowing Donna loved it when the baby came here.

Sara looked at the dress. "It's beautiful. What do you think, Donna?"

"I think it is beautiful."

"Thank you. What do you think about us having a double wedding?"

"Do you want to get married again?"

"I have wanted to. But this is Cassie's wedding."

"Sara, nothing would make me happier than to walk down the aisle with you and Daddy. Please say yes."

"Yes, I would love to share your wedding with you and Luca. But what about Luca? Maybe he wants to have a special day with just you."

"Oh, Luca won't care. As long as we get married, that's all he cares about. He wants a ring on my finger. He's afraid I will start back on my traveling nurse job. I would never leave him, Michael, and Donna. I love them too much to go anywhere, and I'm here forever."

I looked over at Donna and saw her wiping her eyes. I went over and hugged her. "I will never stop telling Michael how much his mommy loved him and what a wonderful woman she is."

"I know. I am so blessed that you are raising Michael. I never have to worry about him anymore."

"Knock, knock, hey, here I am," Cheryl said, walking into the room.

"Cheryl, I didn't know you were coming." She looked between us and knew that I had something to do with this little surprise. "I'm so glad you're here," Donna said.

"I couldn't stay away from my sister any longer, and I brought my work with me." She looked at me, "Are you sure it's okay if I stay for a while?"

"Yes, I'm sure. Let's get your things and put them into your room. I already have a room for you. I knew you couldn't stay away from your sister. Thank you so much for my wedding dress. I love it."

We were in Cheryl's room when Luca and Michael came home, carrying a bag of Chinese food. Sara had already gone home. She called and said Ethan was happy she was getting a real wedding. So, everything was all set for the wedding.

"I've asked Sara if she would like to have a double wedding with us."

"I thought Ethan and Sara were already married."

"They are married but had a quick wedding at the airport with an Elvis Presley impersonator marrying them."

"That's right, I remember. So, what does Ethan say about getting married twice?"

"He's happy if it makes Sara happy. Plus, she will wear the wedding dress Mama sent me, and I can wear the one Cheryl made for me."

"Well, that turned out perfectly. Now your mama won't have her feelings hurt."

"That's what I thought. Sara gets a real wedding, and everyone is happy."

17

LUCA

I looked at Ryker like he was crazy. "Why are you asking me to go? Isn't there anyone else? What if I'm not back in time for my wedding?"

"This will take you four days at the most. You're not getting married until the Saturday after this coming Saturday. You have plenty of time to do the job. Everybody else is busy. I have to leave tomorrow for Los Angeles. I have a job I'm doing there."

"You know I don't like Alaska. It's so damn cold."

"It's summertime. It's not cold. All you have to do is pick this guy up, bring him to Portland, and that's it."

"Doesn't this sound a little fishy? Why can't the guy get on the airplane himself? You told me he's thirty-three. Why can't he take a plane on his own?"

"I think he's disabled."

"You should have said that, to begin with. Cassie will not be happy."

"She doesn't have time to be unhappy. She has all those people she takes care of at your house? Here's his file. All you have to do is go to his house, pick him up, and bring him to Portland."

"Okay, I'll be back in a couple of days. I'll tell Cassie what's going on and then head out."

"I promise you will have plenty of time to return before your wedding."

"I better have."

I walked to our house. If Cassie didn't like the idea, she could take it up with him. I walked inside my house, and I could hear singing. *Is that Cassie? I didn't know she could sing.* I stood there and watched her as she mopped the floors and sang.

"Where's the cleaning lady?"

"She called in sick. We need to give her a raise. She has all of us here now, and the house isn't as clean as it was when it was just you. What do you think about that?"

"I agree. I'll call Sally and tell her that I'm giving her a fifty-dollar per day raise."

"Perfect. Why did Ryker want you? Is he trying to send you off to a job? Did you tell him no?"

"Yeah, that's what he wanted. It'll only take a couple of days. I have to pick a guy up in Alaska and take him to Portland. He's disabled, so he can't do this on his own. I promise I'll be back in a couple of days, long before our wedding."

"You're such a good man. Of course, you have to help this person. When do you leave?"

"In the morning. Where's Michael?"

"He's with my grandpa. They went to get ice cream. I think it's good for him to get out occasionally. I know it's important that he sees his mom as often as he can, but I don't like him cooped up for a long period of time. Donna is sleeping. Cheryl's walking down the beach so that just leaves you and me."

"I don't want you overdoing it, Cassie. I know you're doing this out of the kindness of your heart, but this is a lot to take on. I don't like it when you always have to work."

"I don't work all the time. It's good for me to stay busy. I'm used to doing that. I don't like being idle where I just stand or sit around. I like something to keep me busy. I'm going for a run after dinner. Would you like to go with me?"

"Try keeping me away."

∼

How far in the woods is this place? I better come to it soon or I'm going to have to walk. The damn road is disappearing. I think I see some smoke from the chimney. Hopefully, this is his house.

I went around a bend in the road, and this beautiful house stood right there in front of me, looking as regal as a queen's castle.

I parked the truck and saw the man on the front porch. I knew who he was right away. Tag Harris, a famous baseball player; I wondered what had happened to him. "Hello, Tag. So, this is where you've been hanging out."

"Yep, this is where I'm hanging out. It took you long enough. Did you get lost?"

"No. I left this morning, and here I am. Why did you want me here before today?"

"I called two days ago."

"Who did you talk to?"

"I don't remember who I talked to. Besides, it doesn't matter anyway. It's not like I have someplace to go."

"Well, you are going to Portland. What's in Portland?"

"I have another house there. So, you know what I am doing now? I go from house to house."

"I thought you were married."

"I was married. She didn't want to stay with a crippled ex-baseball player."

"You are better off without her."

"I go to court next week and she wants my money. I can't make it without money because I can't do anything for myself. I have to figure out how I'm going to make money."

"Wait until your divorce is completely over and then you can write a book. You can go all over the place. Why? Every television station out there will want you. They will want to interview you about your book. And I know just the person to help you write your book. Her name is Donna Winters. She's at my house right now. Why don't we go there first."

"Is she your girlfriend?"

"No, my lady is Cassie. I'm getting married soon. Donna is the mother to my son, Michael. Cassie is caring for her because she has cancer and hasn't much time left."

"Then how will she help me with a book?"

"I think this would help to keep her mind busy. Plus, it'll give you something to do."

"Damn, you want me to go to your house and write a book, and publish it after the divorce is final so my ex-wife can't take one penny from it."

"Yes, that's what I'm saying. What do you say?"

"I say let's go. Damn, I'm actually looking forward to something. This is the first time since the car accident that my heart is pumping fast again. So where should I start in the book?"

"I would think you would start when you were driving home after your last game, and that car hit you head-on."

"I wasn't driving."

"Who was?"

"My soon-to-be ex-wife."

"Oh, this will be interesting. I can see everyone who

loves baseball running to buy this book." I loaded his suitcase into the vehicle, and we left. "How did you find this place in the middle of nowhere?"

"This was my parents' property, they didn't do anything with it, so I bought it from them and built my home here. I like my solitude. I enjoy my own company. I enjoy reading. So, are we driving back to Oregon or flying?"

"What do you want to do?"

"Let's drive."

"Drive it is."

It took us two days to drive home. When we pulled into the driveway, I saw Cassie running up from the beach. She smiled, seeing me. She kissed me as I got out of the car. "Sweetheart, I want to introduce you to someone."

She bent her head and looked into the car. "Tag, you were Luca's job?"

"Yes, wait, are you marrying Luca?"

"I better be because he just kissed me." She walked to the back of the truck and pointed her finger at the wheelchair. I got it out and watched as she pushed it to Tag's side. She helped him into it like she'd done it a hundred times.

"Where do you two know each other from?"

"Cassie and Sara were my nurses for three months while I was recovering from the accident. Is Sara here as well?"

"I have so much to tell you," Cassie said, walking on the side of the wheelchair. "Remember we told you about our family, the mafia."

"Yes, I remember that story. I told you it must have been a lie. What did you do?"

"Well, Sara…"

"Don't you want to know why Tag is here?" I asked, interrupting her.

"Of course, I do. Why are you here?"

"I'm going to write a book about my accident and my disability, and Luca said he has someone who will help me. Her name is Donna."

"Donna," Cassie said, frowning.

"Yes, Donna used to be a publisher and editor with a big publishing company. I thought this would keep her mind busy."

She threw her arms around me. "You are the best person I know."

"I thought it was strange that he would have his ex-girlfriend living here with his newfound son, but now that I know who he's marrying, it doesn't surprise me at all."

"Sara is married."

"Really? You two have been busy."

"She'll be here for dinner tonight. My grandfather and my parents will be here. Let's not tell Sara that you are here. We'll surprise her."

"Cassie, is that nice? Don't you remember she fell in love with me? At least that's what she said," Tag said, laughing.

"If you thought that was funny, she was drinking wine and asked Ethan to marry her. He wouldn't let her take it back. I'm going to shower while Luca shows you to your room. Give him the one next to Donna."

"This is going to be so exciting. You can ask me anything you don't remember about your accident and how Priscilla acted. I have a photogenic memory."

He watched as Cassie walked upstairs for her shower. You are one lucky son-of-a-bitch." Tag said, watching her disappear up the stairs.

"Don't I know it?"

"So, who did Sara marry?"

"Ethan Sullivan. He's also a former SEAL. We all work together in SEAL Security. They have a child. Let me show you your room. You have an attached bathroom and shower. If you need anything, let me know. I'm going to run upstairs and shower.

When I came back downstairs, Tag and Donna were talking. "Cassie introduced me to Donna and Cheryl. Your son looks just like you."

"I know, he's terrific. Did he recognize you?"

"Yes, I already signed his baseball."

I heard someone at the front door and smiled to myself. The family had arrived. When Sara saw Tag, she handed the baby to Ethan and screamed as she ran over and hugged him. He pulled her onto his lap and laughed. "Where is your husband?"

"Why don't you get off Tag's lap, wife." We all heard her giggle. Then she pulled Ethan and Baby Dante over and introduced them to Tag. Next, her parents and grandfather were introduced to Tag.

"Is Tag your nickname?" Grandpa asked.

"Yes, it's short for Taggert. When I was a kid, my sister called me Tag, and it stuck."

"What are you doing here?"

"I'm going to write a book, and Luca said Donna would be a big help. It was actually Luca who suggested that I write a book."

Sara laughed and hugged Luca, "You are as bad as Cassie and me."

"Is this your baby boy that Cassie was telling me about? He's beautiful."

"Thank you. We love him so much." She looked around for Cassie, who was talking to Donna and Cheryl. I watched Sara put her arm through her mom's, and they walked over to Cassie, and we guys went outside.

18

CASSIE

"Mama, I'm so glad we found you. I never dreamed I would have a wedding like this with everyone I love here."

"It will be the most beautiful wedding I've ever seen. Now, I'm going to get Sara so she can be here when your dad comes to walk you two down the aisle."

My mom was not exaggerating when she said it was beautiful. Not all of our friends could make it. Some were working overseas.

My mom came in with Sara. Both of us started to cry when we saw each other. "Both of you are going to have mascara all over your faces."

I laughed when I saw Sara and her raccoon eyes. "Why are we wearing makeup? Here," I said, handing her a makeup remover towelette. We cleaned our faces and smiled at each other. I Heard someone singing and realized Gabby was singing at our wedding.

My dad walked into where we were. He wiped his eyes and held his arms out. He wrapped those big strong arms around us. "I love you two more than anything. I am so blessed to have you back in our lives. Are you ready to get married?"

"Yes," we said. Sara took one arm, and I took the other.

"Change places. Your men are on the opposite side." We hurried and switched sides. Both of us giggled.

"I love you, Sara. I'm so lucky you are my sister and my best friend."

When we left the room, I looked where Luca and Michael were; tears fell down my face. I tried to cry beautiful silent tears, but I never was one for crying silently. I was sniffing. Jenna, Luca's beautiful sister, stopped everything and brought me some Kleenex. I hugged her and blew my nose and wiped my eyes. I loved his sisters; they promised to visit us often.

I looked at Grandpa, and he wiped his eyes. My mom was standing, and I saw her shoulders shaking. There had never been a wedding like mine and Sara's. We said our vows, and then everyone congratulated us. Luca didn't leave my side.

"Luca, let me get you something to eat."

"We'll both go," Luca said, kissing me again. "Don't forget this is our wedding night, and I can't wait to get you alone."

I laughed. "We are alone every night."

"Yes, but those nights were not my wedding night. This night is special because we are man and wife. I love you so much that I want to go to bed now."

"Me too, let's leave." I stood on my tiptoes and kissed my husband.

"But this is our house, and we can't leave."

I shook my head. "How is it you can make me forget

where we are? We have to visit with our friends and family, and I'm hungry."

"Me too," Luca growled into my neck. He pulled me to him as a slow song played in the background. I knew what he was hungry for, and it wasn't food. I looked around at everyone. I have so many new friends and would never have to move; this is my permanent home.

∼

"You have to leave? But we are still on our honeymoon."

"The guys wanted me to tell you that your honeymoon is over. They said you couldn't use that excuse anymore. Because it's been three weeks, and we still haven't gone on an actual honeymoon."

I laughed out loud because I wondered when the SEALS would tell me the honeymoon was over. "Where are you going?"

"Tennessee, a man has an ex-girlfriend who killed his dog, and she hired someone to kill him."

Nothing surprised me anymore. I've met a lot of crazy people in this world. I shook my head. "Why does she want him dead?"

"Apparently, he promised to marry her, and she looked forward to having all that money when they married. He found out that she was lying about everything. His brother had her investigated. I guess a friend of his said he knew her from another state. When he broke up with her, she wasn't happy. The guy she tried to hire called the police, but she hired someone else.

"They broke into his house and thought they had killed him, but he lived. Now she has more than one hit out on him. Whoever kills him wins. We have Leo and Jackson hunting with the police and the FBI."

"Wow, she's crazy. What do they win?"

"They are just the winners. I don't think they win anything. We are taking him to Tag's home in Alaska until they find the woman or the hit men. I don't know when I'll be back. There are three of us going—Ethan, Noah, and me."

"I hope they find her, and those hit men fast. I already miss you."

"Listen, sweetheart; Tag will be here if you need anything. Tell him. I know he is in a wheelchair, but still deadly."

"Deadly, you make it sound like he was a SEAL."

"He was. He wasn't on our team, but his team was badass."

"Wait, are you saying he played baseball and was a Navy SEAL?"

"Yes, he was. Tag played college baseball. Then he joined the SEALS. He was in the service until he went back to baseball until the accident."

"Okay, that's good to know. Does he carry a gun? If he does, it has to be locked in a safe. I don't want Michael getting anywhere near it. Did you tell Michael that you were leaving?"

"I'm going to tell him now. Sweetheart, tell me why you're upset. You know this is my job and what I have to do."

"I know. I don't want those hit men anywhere around you, so be careful."

"I will be very careful. You don't have to worry about me, sweetie. Nobody knows about Tag's house way out in the boonies. I'm going to find Michael and tell him goodbye."

Michael and I told Luca goodbye. And then we made homemade pizza together. It was so fun. We laughed because flour was all over us. Donna and Tag were busy writing his book. Our house became our home where we loved to be.

19

LUCA

Two weeks later, I was ready to leave this amazing house in all of its beauty. I didn't care about the inside heated pool and sauna any longer. Mark didn't like us watching his every move. But as long as we were guarding him, we would do that. He was still pissed off at himself for letting that woman fool him.

He hated to think what would have happened if he had married her. Thank God his brother investigated her. They would have been married, and he would be dead by now. I'm sure she would have fed him poison. We were surprised when we saw who his brother was. I think he was with Tag's SEAL team. His name is Oliver Steele.

"Tag is at my house right now. This is his home."

"I heard about his accident. That makes me so angry. After everything he went through as a SEAL, he has an accident that cripples him. How is he doing?"

"He's writing a book right now. We have someone in our house helping him with the book. I'm actually glad he's there. My wife and my son are there, I know Tag can protect them."

"Why do you think they need protection?"

I laughed out loud. "It's not so much that they need the protection. My wife, Cassie, always seems to get involved in some unsafe stuff. She's busy right now because she has Donna, Tag, and Michael to keep her busy. Plus, Grandpa's there for a few more weeks."

"Who's your grandpa?"

"Marlon Rissi."

"As in Marlon Rissi, Italian mob?"

"That was untrue. None of that gossip is true about Marlon. He's a sweet grandpa who loves his family. Don't ever tell him I said he was sweet."

Oliver chuckled. "Okay, I won't tell him."

"How's Mark doing? Will he let you change his bandages?"

"Yeah, I've already changed them. He doesn't like me changing them. But he can't reach his back, can he? He's angry at himself because he let a pretty face trick him. Just glad I figured it out before they got married. He'd be dead right now."

"Yeah, that was lucky," I said, patting him on his back. "I'm going to walk the perimeter. Make sure everything is safe and locked down for the night. I don't know how anyone can find this house anyway. There's no reason to connect him and Tag. He knows not to use his phone. He knows he can't talk to anybody outside this property. No one will find us out here."

Oliver followed me outside.

"I wonder if they're having any luck finding any of the people she hired. It's been two weeks. You would think they would find someone. I'm sure that woman isn't that hard to find. I mean all the underground junkies who need money know where she is. Why not just ask one of them?"

"From what Noah said, she contacts everyone from a computer. Noah's wife, Sofie, is a genius with a computer. And she's trying to find everything she can about the hits. Now that they know it's coming from a computer, it won't take long for Sophie to find where it's coming from."

My phone rang, and I looked down and saw it was Sofie. I smiled at the fact that I'd just called her name and here she was calling me. "Hey, Sophie, what's up?"

"We have the location of the woman. The FBI is arresting her as we speak. We'll have to wait and see if she talks."

"Is there a reason to believe she won't?"

"We don't know that yet. I'll call you back when the FBI contacts me."

"Thanks, Sophie. I'm glad you are on our side."

"You're welcome. I tried calling Noah, but he wasn't answering his phone."

"Why wouldn't he be answering his phone?" I turned around and looked at Oliver. "Let's find Noah." We hurried inside and found Ethan. "Have you seen Noah?"

"No, I haven't seen him in about forty-five minutes. Why do you think he's missing?"

"Sophie called. She said they arrested the woman, but she couldn't get a hold of Noah. That's why she called me. They don't know if the woman's going to talk or not. Since she's got these free hits and everybody just wants to be the winner, they don't think she's going to say anything."

More important was why Noah would be missing. We all ran up to where Mark was supposed to be. It looked like he was sleeping but I checked him anyway. "Mark, wake up."

"What the hell's the matter?"

"Have you seen Noah?"

"No, I haven't seen him."

"Let's split up. We'll find him faster. Mark, you stick right next to me." Thirty minutes later, we found Noah. He was unconscious, lying in a pool of blood. I picked him up, carried him to the nearest sofa, and called Ethan. "I found him, but he's unconscious. He's been shot."

"Fuck. Who the hell would shoot him?"

"That means somebody's here." I looked at Oliver. "How the hell would someone find out we were here? Nobody knows except us. How could they have found us? And how many are here? Let's lock this place up."

We got our big guns and walked from room to room. I was checking every inch of the house. "The house is too damn big; we won't be able to use it again. There are too many rooms." I checked Noah I found his wound. There was so much blood on the floor that I prayed he still had blood left inside him. He opened his eyes.

"Fuck, someone is here."

I nodded, letting him know we figured that out on our own. "The others are checking the place out to see if they can find anything."

"You mean Oliver and Ethan."

"Yes, Oliver and Ethan. Did you see anything?"

"No, I felt the bullet slam into me, and I remember falling back and hitting my head. You'll have to take the bullet out."

"At least it's not in a dangerous place. We need to all load up in the SUV and go to one of our other safehouses."

I think you're right. When the others get back, we'll leave."

"Aren't you going to get the bullet out first?"

"Yes, this won't take any time." I ripped his shirt to see where the bullet went in his shoulder and out the other side.

"Did you have to rip my shirt?"

"It's no good anymore, it's covered in blood. Great news. The bullet went all the way through your shoulder." I took a tee shirt out of his bag. We had already gathered our bags and put them in the living room. I put it on him and then I checked his head.

"Wow, you got a big knot here on the back of your head." I called Ethan, "We'll leave as soon as you get back here."

"We found footprints. It looks like there are at least three people. Make sure Mark isn't anywhere they can get a clear shot of him."

"He's not," I said, looking down at Mark. He was sitting on the floor with his back to the sofa, and me standing over him.

"Do I really need to be under you?"

I heard Noah chuckle. "If you want to live, this is where you must be. Look at Noah; he's been shot. Someone's here, and we don't know where they are now. Ethan said that they found three sets of footprints. As soon as he gets back here, we're leaving."

When Ethan and Oliver returned, we went to the garage and climbed into the vehicle. I wondered where the shooters disappeared to. "Hold up a minute," I said, bringing us to a halt. "Why are they not here? If they're not here, where are they? Could they be waiting for us to pull out of the garage and then they'll let the bullets fly?"

Noah nodded, and then he grabbed his head. "This is why I like cameras all around the property. We would have cameras if we were at any of our safe houses. Wait, I have my drone in my pack. I'll fly it over the property and see where they are. Can you get it out for me?"

We all sat in the vehicle as Ethan flew the drone overhead. We saw the men with guns waiting for us down the dirt road. "They are waiting for us to drive by so they can spray our vehicle with bullets. Won't they be surprised when we spray them with bullets instead?"

"Mark, you are staying here with Noah. We'll be right back. This won't take any time at all."

The drones showed two men on one side of the road and one on the other. Oliver and Ethan went to one side. I went to the other. While their eyes were glued on the road, we snuck behind them. I raised my hand. And then I said, "Hello." They jumped so high and then we shot them.

I called the police. We had to wait until they came out there. We explained everything to them, then jumped in the vehicle and went to another safe house. We drove, so it took longer. We went to our safe house in Arizona.

We were there for another three weeks. And then we moved to another safe house in Missouri. We got a call that they had found the woman. But we had to wait and see if there was going to be anyone else trying to kill him before we took him home.

"How long will Tag be at your house?" Oliver asked.

"I'm not sure. Donna is helping him with the book. But she has cancer. She only has a few months to live. So, I don't know what's going to happen with that. If I ever get a chance to call my wife again, I can ask her some questions. It's been almost two months and I haven't seen or talked to her."

"I thought maybe I would come by and see him."

"Sure. Will he likes seeing you?"

"The last time we saw each other, we got into a big fight."

"I felt bad about it. I haven't talked to him since."

"Oh yeah, what did you fight over?"

"We were in Afghanistan. I found some alcohol. Tag told me to go to bed and sober up, instead of doing what I should have done. I punch him in the face. He beats the piss out of me. The next day we were attacked. Tag was shot while he ran to save some kids."

"Why did you get drunk in a war zone?"

"I was doing something stupid. My fiancée broke up with me. Because she said she didn't want to be married to someone who thought more of his Navy Seal buddies than he did of her. I was angry because she had broken up with me. But when I sobered up, I realized it was the truth. By that time, they had already taken Tag off in a helicopter. That was the last time I saw him."

My phone rang and I jumped. I looked down. It was Ryker. "Please tell me you're calling to say I can go home."

"Sorry, not yet. They are trying to plead with the woman to see how many people she has out there to kill her ex-boyfriend. So, I just wanted you guys to know that she claims she doesn't know how many people there want to kill him. She said it went all haywire, and people made it into a bet who would win even though there is nothing to win.

"Now it's become a competition of who can kill him first. The only way this will be fixed is that Mark will have to pay them not to kill him. We will splash this all over the newspapers so that everybody will know the woman is locked up and there won't be a winner."

"I've never heard of anyone doing hits for free. Somebody's giving them money. If it's not her, then who is it? I'm going to talk to Mark. I'll call you back."

"You think maybe there's someone else wanting him dead?"

"He's extremely wealthy. Who else would benefit from him being dead?" I felt Oliver staring at me. "Who would benefit from Mark dying?"

"Let's ask him who is in his will, and then we will find the person who hired the hits."

Mark was sitting out by the pool. "Why are you two looking at me like that?"

"Who will become rich when you die?"

"Sharon and David. Why?"

"Because we now know who hired the hits."

"Sharon and David wouldn't have me killed."

"They know what is going on with you. Did you tell them about Alaska?"

"Wait, let me think. Fuck! Those mother fuckers. I am a fucking idiot. Let's set them up. I want both of them behind bars. I'm going to call and tell them where I am."

He got up and walked into his room. Then he came out with his phone. He held his hand up and made his call. "Hey, how are you doing? Don't let Oliver know I'm using my phone. I'm not allowed to tell anyone where I am. I know I can trust you."

"Mark, I've been worried sick about you. Where are you? They caught Kathleen weeks ago. When is this going to be over?"

"From what I understand the bad guys decided this was a game and whoever kills me is the winner. They don't even have to be paid money. It's all about the game now; they want to be the winner."

"That sounds so scary. I hope they don't find you. Where are you?"

"We are in Sedona, Arizona. It's really beautiful here. When this is over, I'm buying a home here. I better go. I love you, Aunt Sharon."

"We love you too, sweetie."

"It's your aunt?"

"My aunt and uncle. On my mother's side. Sharon is my mom's youngest sister. Oliver has a different mother. My parents died in a train accident a couple of years ago. Oliver's mother is still living. Our father is who the money came from."

"When the accident happened, Sharon and Dave came and visited Mark. I never liked either of them. I've told Mark a million times something was wrong with those two. Now I'm fucking going to kill them."

"Do they know you have them in your will?"

"Hell, yes, they know, and now that I think about it, I am convinced they were putting something in my drinks. I bet they are living in my house right now. God, I am so stupid. Why didn't I listen to you," Mark said, looking at Oliver.

"What are we going to do?"

"We'll wait until they get here, and then we'll have the police here waiting for whoever shows up. I'll have the police pick up your relatives. The ones that show up will tell us who hired them. Then it will be over."

Two days later, they came. There were four of them. We all waited in a dark house and left the front door unlocked. When they came inside, the lights went on. And the three men and one woman stood there in shock when they saw all the guns pointed at them. They dropped their weapons.

"Wait, we are here to help you. Did you think we were here to harm you? No, no, we came to help you." The woman tried walking to where Mark stood, looking down at her.

"Get the fuck away from me." He looked at the men, "How much did she promise you?"

"A million dollars. She also wanted your brother killed. She said he would make sure she never got a penny of his money. So we had to kill him as well."

The woman tried attacking Mark, and then a man grabbed her. "This is all your fault. I didn't want anything to do with any of this. But you wouldn't stop." He looked at

Mark, "Your mother would send money weekly so that Sharon would leave her alone. When she died, so did Sharon's bank. It drove Sharon crazy not having all that nice stuff. If you don't lock her up for good, she's crazy enough to kill you herself."

"Shut up, you stupid bastard; I didn't see you turning any of that down." Then she grabbed a gun and pointed it at Mark. A bullet hit her between the eyes.

I looked around, and a police officer was putting his gun back. "Lock all of them up and get her out of here." Twenty minutes later, it was over.

"You can go home whenever you want. We caught the ones who were after you. Hopefully, you can move on with your life."

I didn't want to be rude, but I was ready to return home to my wife. I couldn't wait to call her. But I knew this was upsetting for him. Fuck, it was his aunt and uncle who wanted him dead. I wanted to go home to Cassie.

20

CASSIE

My pie was burning, Michael was crying, and the phone started to ring. I didn't know what to do. I shut the oven off, took Michael by the hand, and pulled him onto my lap as I sat in a chair. The phone rang again, and I saw it was Luca.

"Luca, I'm so happy to hear your voice. Please, tell me you get to come home soon."

"I'll be there in a couple of hours. Tell me what's wrong."

"Michael needs his daddy." I tried not to cry; I knew he could hear the tears in my voice. "I'm going to let you speak to him. He's right here in my lap." I could hear their conversation, and I wanted to cry.

"Michael, I'm on my way home, honey, tell me what's going on."

"Mom is at the hospital. I'm scared she won't get to come home."

"Sweetheart, you know your mommy is sick. One day, she will go to heaven. Remember what we talked about."

"Yes, but I don't want her to go to heaven yet. She was going to tell me a story."

"I know, honey; maybe she will still tell you a new story. When I get home, I'll tell you a story. I love you, Michael. Let me talk to Cassie.

"I love you, Daddy." He handed me the phone and leaned back against me.

"Sweetheart, is it that bad?"

"I don't know. She wanted to go to the hospital, so we called an ambulance. That was an hour ago. Sara was going to the hospital to see what this was all about. She wasn't any sicker than when she came here. I thought she was getting better. Helping Tag with his book was helping her. She laughed more, and she seemed to enjoy working on the book. I can't wait for you to get home. I love you."

"I love you, sweetheart; I'll see you in a few hours."

"Okay, I'm sorry I didn't ask about your client."

"I'll tell you about it when I get home. Goodbye, darling."

"Okay. See you soon."

I hung up the phone and wrapped my arms around Michael.

"Cassie, I'm glad you are my other mom. I love you."

"I love you too, sweetheart."

I carried him up to bed. It was nap time. I lay there with him, and Luca was there when I opened my eyes. I got up and he held me in his arms. Then we walked down the hall to the kitchen.

"Luca, I missed you so much..."

The phone rang, and Luca answered it, "Sara, I'm glad to be home also. What's going on with Donna? ... Okay, I'll let Cassie know what's going on."

Luca looked at me. "They don't know anything yet. She says they'll know something in a couple of hours. Why don't we start dinner, and we can relax and when Michael wakes up, it will be normal here? Maybe it'll take his mind off his mom."

"That's a great idea. We're having tacos tonight."

"I love tacos."

"Me too." He pulled me onto his lap and started nuzzling my neck.

"I can't wait until tonight. You and I are going to make love all night long. I've been dreaming about this night... Oh yeah, you taste good. How about we go to our room and forget about cooking for another hour?"

"I think that's a great idea. You must have been reading my mind."

"Or were you reading mine?" We walked up the stairs to our room. Luca had my clothes off before I even knew what he was doing. I looked at his beautiful body. He looked like he could advertise for any muscle man magazine.

He was beautiful. I saw the bullet wounds on his chest. My hand trailed down both of the scars, and I kissed them. Luca picked me up, and I wrapped my legs around him as his lips took mine. His kiss made me want to cry. I loved this man so much. If a kiss could make me cry, I needed help.

"I love you," he whispered against my neck.

"I love you so much. I worry about you. Now that I see the bullet wounds, I'm more worried. I never really thought much about your job until today. I see how dangerous it is. Knowing Noah was shot brought it home to me how dangerous it is."

"Sweetheart, it's not always like this. We were saving a man from crazy people who turned out to be his family. It's hardly ever like this."

I didn't believe him but I let it go for now. Luca had us both undressed, and I wanted him. I wanted his hardness inside me.

"I want you hard and fast. We only have a little time before Michael wakes up. Hurry, give it to me." Luca chuckled at that. He pushed his hard erection inside me and moved so fast it was making me crazy, I begged for all of it. When I orgasmed, I cried. Luca kept going, giving me more and more. My body was on fire. I orgasmed again, and then Luca had his release.

"Why are you crying?" He kissed my tears and my mouth. He kissed my closed eyes. He kissed my neck.

"I don't know why; it's just that I love you. I'm a little shaken up. Making love with you does that to me. Ignore me. I'm being silly."

"You're never silly." He pulled me on top of him, "I will love you for the rest of my life."

"I will love you forever. Now, I need to get up before Michael wakes up."

We got up and jumped in the shower. We laughed as we made love in the shower, trying to hurry. By the time Michael woke up, we were cooking dinner.

"Where is Tag?"

"He went to talk to his lawyer. He heard from someone back home that his wife had been fooling around with multiple men before the accident. He said she would not get a penny of his money. He said he would be back in a week or two."

"Daddy, you're home," Michael said, running to Luca. "I missed you."

"I missed you too. We are having tacos for dinner."

"I love tacos. Did you talk to Mom?"

"No, not yet. Aunt Sara says she's staying at the hospital tonight. After they put her into a room, we'll call and talk to her. She will be back here tomorrow. I don't want you worrying about her. You know she is sick. We brought her here so you could be with her longer. But she's still sick."

"I don't want her to be sick anymore."

"None of us want her to be sick. I wish she wasn't, but she is, and there is nothing you or I can do about it."

"I know."

"Tell me what you've been doing since I've been gone?"

"Tag was teaching me how to draw. He can draw lots of things. I helped Cassie cook, and Mom is going to help me write a book like she is helping Tag."

"It sounds like you've been busy."

"I've been having lots of fun. There are lots of kids that live around here. Gabby has kids. Lucy has lots of kids. I went to the movies with Tag. Cassie and I went swimming in the ocean.

Cassie said I couldn't go in the ocean without a grown-up. She says it is too dangerous."

"Cassie is right. It is too dangerous."

The phone rang, and I picked it up. "How are you feeling? Michael has been so worried about you. Are you staying the whole night? You'll be home tomorrow, that's good. Yes, he wants to talk to you. Here he is." I handed the phone to Michael and let him talk to his mom.

Luca looked at me. "Did she say anything?"

"No, she said they are going to do some test on her," I whispered because I didn't want Michael to hear us talking about Donna. "I don't know if us bringing her here has made it worse for her and Michael. Before, both of them seemed to accept that she was dying and only had a short time left. Now I'm not sure how they are handling it."

"But since they came here, and she's been doing so well, I think she wants to live longer. I don't think she wants to accept it anymore. I think when she wanted to go to the hospital, it was to see how much the cancer had spread."

"I knew this was going to be hard. Have you talked to Cheryl?"

"I called her as soon as Donna left for the hospital. She's going to be here tomorrow."

"How long has Donna's stomach been burning?"

"It's not just her stomach. She told me she could feel the heat throughout her entire body."

"Do you think that means it's spreading faster?"

"I don't know. I hope not. When we met Donna, she had maybe six months. Of course, no one but God knows how long you'll be on earth. We'll have to wait and see. I'm anxious to see what is going on with her."

I looked at Luca, still whispering so Michael couldn't hear. "She's been doing so good," I shook my head, trying not to cry. "She loves helping Tag with his book. I can hear them laughing together."

"I think we did wrong bringing her home with us. It's not good for you or Michael. Now it's going to be harder on Michael when she dies."

"We'll be here for him. I promise it wasn't wrong to bring her here. She only has Cheryl, and she was almost out of money. We did the right thing; I won't think differently."

"I hope you are right."

"I am."

"Mom is coming home tomorrow. I'm so happy she's coming home." He sat at the table and cried. "I'm not supposed to cry because I'm a big boy now."

Luca picked him up and sat down with him. "Michael, it's okay to cry. I cried at my wedding. It doesn't mean you are a baby if you cry. Do you think I'm a baby?"

"No, you're strong and big. I'm going to be just like you."

"Well, then, it's okay to cry. You can always come and tell me about your feelings. I am always here for you."

"I know because you love me. I'm your son."

"That's right. I will always love you. Your mom will always love you."

21

LUCA

I saw the police car drive into the driveway and walked outside. "Can I help you?"

"Are you Luca Thatcher?"

"Yes, I am."

"There was a train accident, and one of the passengers was a Taggart Harris."

"Is he dead?"

"No, he's at the hospital. He's in surgery right now. He wanted me to tell you that his legs hurt like hell."

"His legs? But Tag is disabled. He can't feel his legs."

"That's what he told me to tell you."

"Thank you for coming here to tell me what is going on. I'll go to the hospital right now."

I walked inside and told Cassie what was going on.

"Oh no, is he going to be alright?"

"The officer said he told him to tell me his legs hurt."

"That's not possible. Or is it? You should call Griff to meet you over there."

"I will. Are you going to be alright if I leave?"

"Yes. I'm fine. Let me know what is going on."

"I will." I pulled her into my arms and kissed her. I wished I had done something before letting her bring Donna here. Cassie was way overdoing it. *I'll fix this after I see what is going on with Tag.*

~

Griff pulled into the parking lot at the same time I did. "Now, what were you saying?"

"A policeman came to my house and told me Tag was injured in a train wreck, and he told the police to tell me his legs hurt like hell."

"That would be a miracle if this accident fixed what the other accident caused. Where is he?"

"He's in surgery, I think. Maybe you can go there right now. These doctors don't know what is going on with him."

"That's what I thought."

"I'll wait to hear from you. There is someone else I need to check on." I walked to Donna's room, and I ran into Cheryl. "Hello... Have you talked to her?"

"No, I just got here. We'll go in together."

We walked into the room, and no one was there. "She'll be right back if you want to wait for her," a nurse said as we were about to leave.

"Thanks, we'll wait."

"I wonder what all of this is about?" Cheryl said, wiping her hands down the front of her pants. "I'm right in the middle of the season. I have a show next week, but I don't want to leave it all up to Cassie to take care of things."

"I just got back yesterday, so Cassie has been doing it alone. I think this is too emotional for Cassie. I shouldn't have let Donna move in with us. Now I don't know what to do. I won't do anything until I talk to Donna. Cassie and

Michael are my main priority. They come first before anyone."

"I understand. I agree with you."

We sat in Donna's room until she came back. I was surprised at how good she looked, and I looked over at Cheryl and could tell she was also shocked. She gained weight, and her skin coloring was no longer gray looking.

"Cheryl, Luca, I'm so happy you are here. I have news about my cancer. It would seem that it is in remission again. The test all showed that no cancer showed up in any of the tests. So I'm not going to die. Not right now, anyway. So I can get a house for Michael and me."

My heart started racing, thinking about Michael moving away. "You're taking Michael away from us?"

"No, Luca, I would never do that. I will find a place in town where we can all share Michael."

I looked over at Cheryl, and she was crying. "I'm so happy you are going to live. My God, I need to call Cassie and Michael."

"Can I please be the one to tell them? They are on their way to pick me up. I want to see their reaction and how happy both of them are." She looked at me, "The best thing that has ever happened to me besides having Michael is meeting Cassie. I truly believe she saved my life."

Griff stuck his head inside the room. "Can I talk to you?" I said my goodbyes and went with Griff. "Tag hasn't undergone surgery yet. He wants me to be his surgeon. I want Cassie to help me with the surgery. Can you go get her?"

"She'll be here any minute to pick Donna up. I'll call her and see when she's getting here."

I had gone to check on Tag but I still couldn't see him yet, so I made my way back to Donna's room. I heard Cassie crying as soon as I got to the door and knew she had found out about Donna's cancer. I opened the door and Cassie was wiping her eyes as Michael hugged her.

"Daddy, Mom's not sick anymore," he yelled.

"I know. That's wonderful," I said as I hugged and kissed him. "Cassie, can I talk to you? Cheryl can take Donna and Michael home. Griff needs you to help him with surgery."

She turned and looked at Michael, "I'll see you at home." Then she turned and walked with me to where Griffin stood waiting for us. Griffin Anderson was with us in Afghanistan. He is also a former SEAL. His specialty is spinal injuries. I was hopeful about Tag. "Will they let me in surgery?" Cassie asked.

"You are my assistant. What can they say?"

"Okay, let's go."

I kissed my wife, and then she walked with Griff. "I'll be right here waiting for you, sweetheart."

"Okay, I love you."

I ran up, caught her from behind, turned her around, and kissed her. "I love you."

"Damn it, Luca, let her go. We have surgery right now."

I let her go. "Why is Cassie the one that has to help you?"

"Because she will do what I ask her to do."

Cassie stopped walking. "What are you going to ask me to do?"

"Nothing, don't worry about it. It's not illegal."

I had to smile; everyone loved my wife. My life was perfect. I married the woman I love, and I had a beautiful son. I don't know how my life turned out so great. While I was in prison, I thought I would be there forever, but the truth came out, and I was set free. Just in time to find Cassie in a little town in Ireland, where we would share two unforgettable nights.

Fate brought us together, and we will be together for the rest of our lives.

THE END
KEEP READING FOR MORE OF SEAL SECURITY
GRAYSON BOOK 5

22

GILLY

I cried like a baby in the movie theatre. My blind date kept handing me more Kleenex tissues because the lady behind him passed them to him as fast as if trying to stop water from a spout. She made a noise for me to shut up. All of the people around me, wanted me to be quiet. But I could not stop crying. I had so many people silencing me, I couldn't even begin to tell you how many there were. I could tell my blind date was exasperated with me. But he was the one who picked the movie, so it was all on him.

Now everyone knows why I do not watch sad movies. I cried while watching them or got horrible headaches from trying not to cry. Plus, the tragic film would make me sad for an entire week. Who dies in a romance for crying out loud? I only like happily ever after romance movies, not that I watch much television. I enjoy reading if I have extra time, but I am always busy.

I turned to the guy who was my blind date. He was very handsome in an outdoor strong looking way. He watched me closely, waiting to see if I needed another Kleenex.

"Look, I am ready to leave. I will only cry more, thinking about how this movie will end. So far, I'm pretty sure I know the ending."

"Then why did your grandma tell mine that you love sad movies? Hell, your grandma picked out the movie."

"My grandma died last year. How long have you had this information?" I asked, walking out of the theater. "Besides, I do not watch movies. Why would people say that actors and sports players are heroes? My father was a hero. He died fighting overseas." We stopped in the lobby, and he looked at me, and I looked at him. Damn, I felt that feeling down in my core again, if you know what I mean. When I first laid eyes on him, I felt it. I needed to pull my panties away from me. They were already sticky. He smelled so good. I wanted to tase him.

He pulled out his paper, shaking his head as he read it. "Is your name Gilda Staples? You live at three hundred Fifth Avenue. That's where the taxi took me, so I have the right address."

I sucked on my bottom lip to keep myself from chuckling. *His eyes are beautiful. Keep him.* I chuckled again as that thought popped into my head. "No, my name is Gillian Marshall. I live at three hundred Sixth Avenue. It would seem you picked up the wrong woman."

I couldn't help it. I burst into laughter. At first, he looked at me like I was crazy, but I saw the laughter in those beautiful eyes. I might add his beautiful stormy gray eyes, I felt them suck me closer to him. Then I looked at him. Damn, this guy was hot. He was about six foot two. His dark hair fell onto his forehead. I reached up and moved it to the side. *Stop it right now, Gilly. You do not touch him again. He is not yours!*

His eyes narrowed when he looked at me. "Sorry," I said,

stepping back.

"Then why did you go out with me if you aren't my blind date?"

"Because my blind date's name is Grayson, I assumed you were him when you introduced yourself as Grayson. I figured you were just early."

"Are you telling me he has the same last name as mine?"

"I didn't pay any attention to his last name. Sorry."

"How can this happen?" He looked at me. I still had a grin on my face. I watched as his eyes lit up, and then he started laughing. "Damn, I need to explain what happened to the other woman. I'm sure my grandmother will hear about this from her grandmother."

"Good luck with the other woman. I held out my hand. He put his hand into mine. Heat ran over my body, I tried to block it out. "It was nice meeting you, Grayson."

"Call me Gray. All my friends do. It was nice meeting you too. So, you don't like movies?"

"I watch some, but never this kind. Goodbye."

"Let me take you home." We were on the sidewalk by now.

"I think you better explain to Gilda what happened, or your grandma will let you know how unhappy she is."

Gray nodded, and I started to walk away. He didn't let go of my hand. I turned, and his mouth landed on mine. I knew I should have made him stop, but my arms wrapped around him, they went inside his jacket and gave him a body hug. It wasn't like any kiss I'd ever had. When he raised his head, I swayed. His lips touched mine again, and I took a step back. My body almost tipped to the side. His arm reached out and held on until I got my balance.

I turned and kept walking. I had to get away from this hot-as-hell man. He'd have me a hot mess if I didn't leave. I shook my head. I couldn't believe the man I wanted to go to bed with was my wrong date. I chuckled all the way home. When I got there, a man was sitting on my steps.

"Is your name Grayson?"

"Yes, I wondered if you were standing me up."

I chuckled as I explained what had happened. I couldn't help but compare this Grayson to my other Grayson. *Well, actually, he's not mine. But I can dream. Maybe he'll come by and see me sometime?* The wrong blind date had eyes so gray that they almost looked silver. His hair was thick, and the color was as dark as a raven's wings. His scent would stay with me for many nights. *There I go again, getting my panties in a mess.*

Okay, Gilly, stop right now. He was the wrong date, which is how you will think of him. I wondered how he and his real date were getting along. *That is a chapter in my life that I will close. Maybe I won't. He may come back to see me. I can hope.*

"Have you had dinner yet?"

I have to stop thinking about the other Grayson.

I shook my head, determined to enjoy the rest of my evening. So, what if this guy wasn't six-two with beautiful eyes? He was cute. His eyes were a lovely hazel. So, what if my panties didn't get wet or he didn't disrupt my breathing pattern? "No, I haven't eaten. I would love to go to dinner with you. How about a steak? We have a steak house around the block. We can walk."

"Wonderful, we might make this a memorable night after all. I have to tell you, though, I'm a vegetarian."

"Oh, I can have a chicken salad, that way, you don't have to watch me eat my medium-rare steak."

"Thank you. A lot of women don't care if they cut into the meat while I'm there trying not to watch."

My mind drifted to my wrong date, wondering what he had for dinner.

23

GRAYSON

I wanted to take her bottom lip and suck on it like she was doing. Damn, she was hot. I wondered why she needed a blind date. She must have had the same problem I had with my grandma, who always tried setting me up. Except her grandmother passed away. It must be her friends who set her up. I agreed to go this time, and look where that got me. I had to let my beautiful prize go to her real blind date.

It was harder than hell as I looked into those laughing green eyes as she sucked on that plump bottom lip. I knew if she looked down, she would see my hard erection. Her hair looked like honey-colored silk. It was thick and wavy. I wanted to dig my fingers into it while she lay naked beneath me.

When she moved my hair off my forehead, I almost took those fingers and nibbled on them. I couldn't stop taking that kiss for anything. Her soft lips called to me, and they melted when they touched mine. I ached to touch her entire body. I had to force myself not to taste her neck. She fit me perfectly. *I'll visit her tomorrow and see if she'll have dinner with me.*

Alright, Gray, you can stop daydreaming and see if your date is waiting for you. I know grandma will hear about this. Then what will she say? She will most likely laugh.

I took a taxi to the correct address this time and knocked on the door. An angry woman answered. "Are you my blind date?" she demanded.

"Yes, I'm sorry I'm late," I explained to her what had happened. She laughed, but I noticed it didn't reach her eyes, which weren't emerald or green. But they were a soft brown. "That must have been uncomfortable."

"She laughed it off. I did the same. It's good that she didn't care for the movie, or I would have been later than I am."

"Hmm, I loved that movie. I was so looking forward to seeing it again."

I decided not to take the hint that she wanted to see the movie again. "I heard there is a great steak house not far from here. Why don't we go there for dinner?"

"I know where it is, but I hoped to cook you dinner. I don't particularly like eating other people's food. Please come in. I've already got the salad ready. I'll put the rest of the dinner in the oven. It won't take no time to cook."

What have I gotten myself into?

"Grayson, please make yourself comfortable; you can sit right here," she said, pointing to the head of the table. "I'll make the dressing. I'm making chicken parmesan for our dinner. I didn't realize my grandmother would know my taste in men. I have to be honest with you, I don't sleep with a man on the first date, but I will make an exception with you." She giggled, and I stopped breathing.

NO! My mind shouted. Hell no! "I'm flattered that you

would make me an exception. But I wouldn't sleep with a woman I just met." *I would have slept with Gilly.* "I do not sleep with someone just because I'm dating her. I have to know her before we sleep together."

"Oh, I'm so embarrassed. You must think I'm so forward. Please forgive me."

"No, I don't think that at all." She put the salad in front of me before moving to the other end of the table. *Someone was angry.* I could tell by the way she held herself and the sound my salad plate made hitting the table. *Damn, there is nothing worse than an angry woman.*

I decided to start a conversation to get rid of the uncomfortable silence. I took a bite of the salad and couldn't help the slight cough as I gasped for breath. The salad dressing was lemon and black pepper. I mean pure lemon and lots of black pepper. I tried to pick through the lettuce that looked like it wasn't covered in the dressing and pepper, but the lid must have come off the lemon bottle because my salad was soaked in it. The black pepper was on so heavy I coughed again. I took a drink of water with each bite. When I ran out of that, I took a sip of the wine she poured me and started coughing.

"Are you alright?"

"Yes, excuse me, it went down the wrong side," I said, trying to clear my throat. *What the hell kind of wine is this? I don't think it is wine.* "What kind of wine is this?" I asked, trying to clear my throat.

"Oh, it's not wine. I don't believe in any alcoholic beverage. I served you apple cider vinegar with the mother. It is healthy for you to drink. I always drink it with my dinner."

"Oh." I didn't know what else to say. "Could I please get more water?"

"Yes, I'll get it for you right now. How do you like the

salad? It's my very own dressing recipe. The chicken is also my recipe. I just put a little twist on the parmesan recipe. I'm thinking about writing a cookbook."

"Oh, I'm sure you will get good reviews on it." What's one little lie? I wanted to give her confidence. Maybe she hadn't changed the parmesan too much.

"Thank you. I'll check to see if the chicken is ready."

Is she going to get my water? I guess I'll get it myself. Wait, didn't she just put that in the oven? I got up and went into the kitchen to get some more water. I stopped in the doorway. The woman was a hoarder. There was no available spot in the kitchen. I must have been quiet because it was apparent, she didn't hear me. Her kitchen was filthy. There was garbage everywhere. Dirty dishes were everywhere. She didn't turn around from her task. She took a container from the microwave and poured more vinegar into it. I turned and left before she saw me and returned to the dining room. I chewed my bottom lip, wondering how to get out of eating more of her food.

"It's ready. Here you go," she put a large plate of food in front of me. It was a frigging platter. I knew my eyes bulged, but I couldn't help it. The vegetables were still frozen. I could see the freezer burn on them. I looked at her to see if she was playing a prank on me. I saw a woman with a look that waited for me to say something.

"It looks delicious."

"Thank you. I know you will love it. This is one of my best recipes."

Okay, Gray, you can at least take a few bites. That won't kill you. When I looked up, she waited for me to take the first bite. I didn't know where to take my first bite. I cut a piece of something, I wasn't sure what it was, but I didn't want to eat any chicken because of salmonella. I hoped she couldn't see the small bite on my fork. I quickly popped it into my mouth. I almost choked. The vinegar was so strong. I forced myself to swallow. I knew my eyes must have been watering. I reached for my glass of water, and it was empty. "May I have more water, please?"

"Yes, I'll get it. How is your dinner?"

"It's delicious."

"Thank you."

I watched as she took a bite and then another. Was she going to get my water? I got my glass and stood up.

"Where are you going?"

"To get some water."

"I said I would get it. Here, give it to me."

She jerked the glass out of my hand. I worked fast and dumped most of my food in a container in the corner of the room. The more I looked around, I noticed sheets covered stuff everywhere. There was a walkway from the door to the dining room. How did I not see this before?

"Here you go."

"Thank you, I had a call, and I'm sorry, but I have to leave. My parents are here from out of state and decided to drop in and are now at my house." *What's one lie?*

"That is so rude. Why don't you tell your parents to leave, and you will see them another time? After all, you already screwed up my day. Are you going to make it worse?"

"I'm sorry. I would never treat my parents like that," I stood up and smiled. "Thank you for a wonderful dinner. Good luck with your cookbook." She was frowning. My grandma would get an ear full, and I didn't care.

"Okay, why don't you call me, and we can do something? Maybe it'll be better than this date."

"I'm going to be out of town for a few months, maybe

when I return. I'm always so busy." I was going to the front door when she grabbed my hand. The next thing I knew, she put my hand over her boob.

"Can you feel my heart beating for you?"

To say I was surprised would be almost correct. I had a panic moment. I know that's crazy, but this entire day was crazy—all except when I gazed into the emerald, green eyes of my wrong date and my lips touched hers.

"I loved what little time we had together. Thank you," Gilda raised her face to mine and closed her eyes. I kissed her cheek and got the hell out of there. When I got outside, I took a deep breath of clean air. This was the strangest day I've ever had in my twenty-four years here on earth.

24

GRAY

It'd been eight years since I met Gilly. There'd been a lot of women since that day. My entire life changed that night when I got home. My mom called me and said she needed me to come home. My dad had been taken to the hospital. I called a doctor friend who worked at the hospital in the town where I grew up. First, I called the airport and got a ticket home. Then I called Jack Johnson, my friend. As soon as he answered, he knew why I was calling.

"Gray, your dad isn't doing good. I'm sorry to tell you this, but I'm unsure if he will make it. I saw your family in the waiting room. I told them we were doing everything to save him. Pray, Gray, that's what we need now."

I prayed all the way home. My mom was in ICU with my dad when I arrived. When she saw me, she threw herself into my arms.

"He made it through the surgery," she whispered so Dad couldn't hear. "Now we have to pray he lives. I saw Jack. He said he talked to you. What did he say?"

"He told me to pray. Dad is strong. I know he doesn't

look like it now with all of these wires hooked up to him, but he is. He's going to make it."

My dad lived two months after. He came through, but his heart wasn't strong enough to keep him alive. We took him home, and that's where he died. We talked so much during those two months. We laughed when I told him about my wrong date. He looked sad. I knew he thought I should have gone back and talked to Gilly. And that was what I had planned on doing. But life happens.

I've thought about her many times over the last eight years. My dad was a Navy Seal. I always wanted to be a Seal. My brother Hutch is a Navy Seal. He joined right out of college. I hadn't signed up yet because my mom didn't want me to join the Seals.

When I graduated from college, I moved to the Silicon Valley in California and worked for a High-Tech company. I made a lot of money. I saved it all because my house was paid for and furnished. The company supplied all of that. I never returned to work in the bay area after my dad had his heart attack.

I stayed with my dad. He told me to join the Seals and live life as I wanted. We had long conversations. I wasn't going to leave and miss having a conversation with him. I wanted to spend every moment with him that I could. A couple of my college buddies packed my belongings and brought them to me in Cedar Falls, Oregon. I told them what I planned to do, and they both decided they wanted to join the Seals when I did.

"Here I am eight years later. I left the Seals and worked with my brother and some of our buddies, doing rescue missions. We do a lot of rescues at sea. People get into trouble thinking they can handle their yacht, and a storm comes up out of nowhere, and their boats start sinking. The ocean is vast. Sometimes we can't find them in time. All of us take it very hard if that happens.

This job was deadly if you didn't know what you were doing. That's why my brother was worried about me joining. I'm thirty-four, and he's thirty-six, but he still tries to be my big brother. He said our mom told him she wanted me to settle down and marry. We both laughed over that. Mom has been after both of us to get married. Six months after my dad died, my sister married my friend, Jack. They have three girls, and Jenny is pregnant again. Her having grandkids for mom has kept her off our back.

My brother Hutch looked at me, "Damn, this water is rough. Do you think there are any survivors on the oil rig?"

"If there is, I hope we find them fast. The caller said the rig was being inspected when the storm came up, and there was a fire."

"Listen, Gray. I know this is your specialty, but Mom would kill me if anything happened to you."

"Mom knows how careful I am. So, I don't want you to worry."

The large Navy ship made a deep dip as a giant wave hit us. We bought this vessel from the Navy when they would have to dock it for good. When you have friends in high places, that's what happens. You get to pick your vessel. We did all the maintenance and ensured it was always ready to go out in an emergency.

"I see it!" Gabe Steller shouted.

I ran up top. I could see the fire; all I could think of were burned bodies. I've seen it before when I had to rescue people from a rig on fire. Sweat broke out all over my body.

My brother shook his head. "We're going to abort this rescue. We all agreed that we would abort if it were too dangerous, and I'm the one that calls it. Let's get the hell out of here."

"Hutch, we can't. They might all be alive waiting for us."

"This isn't going to happen. It's too dangerous. I don't want you anywhere on that rig."

I threw my hands in the air. I was ready to throttle my brother. Sometimes he still treated me like his little brother. "Hutch, I can do it. Gabe will be with me. We are all dressed up and ready to go. Come on, Gabe, let's do this." We climbed inside the cage, and Hutch lowered us to the burning platform. The fire was on the other side. We needed to hurry. When it dangled over the offshore platform, I opened the cage door, and we jumped out.

"Can you hear me?" Hutch asked.

I waved my hand to let him know I heard him. We ran to the door and opened it. Damn, it was hot inside. "Stay close to me," I said to Gabe as we ran down the stairs into the burning rig from hell. The storm was so loud I couldn't hear anything. Then I heard a hammering sound. I stopped and looked at Gabe. "Do you hear that?"

"Yes, it's coming from over there." We ran to a closed door. My gloved hand hovered over the knob briefly before I pulled it open. Both of us stood back behind the door as I jerked it open. There were about twelve men there.

"Let's get the hell out of here!" I shouted. "Follow Gabe." I would stay in the back in case someone fell. I saw a woman stumble. *What the hell is a woman doing here?* I saw a man turn to see if she was still behind him. I walked up to her and picked her up. She felt perfect in my arms, and I had the strangest feeling.

"Please put me down. I assure you I can walk."

"The smoke is getting thick. We need to hurry before this entire platform explodes. I ran up the steps three at a time. Gabe had already started loading the men into the cage. I walked over and put the woman inside it.

"Why is a woman out here in the middle of the fucking ocean?" Gabe shouted.

"I'm the fucking inspector." I heard Gabe chuckle at the same time I did.

The cage swung out over the rough waves. As the cage dangled out to sea, a massive wave slapped against it. I held my breath and kept my fingers crossed that the door stayed closed. I saw the woman holding the latch so it couldn't open. It took four trips before we were all on the ship. I threw some sweats and a tee shirt at Hutch. "Can you give these to the woman? I'm sure she's freezing."

"Yeah, I'll show her where the shower is."

25

GILLY

My teeth were chattering when someone handed me a towel, sweats, and a man's tee shirt. "Thank you."

"My name is Hutch Campbell. Follow me. I'll show you where the shower is."

I looked at him. "You remind me of someone."

"I have one of those faces," he said, smiling.

"No, it's your eyes. I'll remember. I have a memory like an elephant." I held onto the rails in the long hallway as we walked. The sea was rough. I had to hold on to the hand bars to keep myself from falling. The ship was huge, but it still rocked. I knew the guy was watching my body as we walked. That was the problem with having so many curves. Men thought they had the right to look. "This storm came out of nowhere. I'm surprised you were able to find us."

"We have excellent equipment for that. It looks like you might have an injury on the back of your leg." Okay, maybe he wasn't looking at my body. He was still talking.

"We do a lot of rescues on rigs. The oil companies make

sure we have the best equipment. They don't want bad publicity. Here you go. The hot water will last ten minutes per shower. When you finish, we'll throw your clothes in the washer, so you can have your own clothes to wear. My brother's clothes will swallow you up. There is shampoo in there, also. I advise you to use that first before the hot water runs out.

"Thank you." I looked around and didn't waste time getting out of my clothes. I took my underclothes into the shower with me to wash them. I'll hang them to dry when I'm assigned a room. I was not letting anyone wash my underwear. I'll stuff them in my bag for now. I hurried through washing my hair then I washed all the salt water off my body. When the water turned cold, I turned it off and dried myself on a large towel. The man was right. His brother's clothes did swallow me. *I'll hang on to them, so they don't fall.* When I opened the door, someone stood there waiting for me.

"I'll show you to your room. One of the guys told us you were all in that room for two days. I'm sure you're hungry and tired. My name is Gabe. Hutch said you might have an injury to your leg. If you need someone to look at it, one of our buddies is a doctor. We'll have him check it out."

"It's nice to meet you, Gabe. I think my leg is fine, but I'll get it checked out. Thank you for asking. Some of the guys got angry because I made them stay in that room for two days. I knew they would die if I didn't make them stay there.

"We were lucky there was a toilet connected to the room. They would have been swept out to sea if they had left the room. We needed to keep the fire under control. The fire would have spread so fast if they had started opening doors. Oil was everywhere. It would have engulfed that rig before they knew what was happening. No one would have made it out of there alive.

"We lost one man when he panicked and ran to the top, trying to stay away from the fire. Now someone will have to tell his family. I've had to do that before, and it's not something I want to do again." We entered a cafeteria. Most of the crew was there eating.

"I'm sorry someone died. Take a seat, and I'll fix you a plate."

I was sitting in the cafeteria corner when someone sat down across from me. I looked up, then I smiled.

"Hello, Gilly."

I turned my head, and there he was, the man I'd thought of him so many times. That one kiss, I'll never forget it. "Grayson, I've often wondered what happened to my wrong date."

"I joined the Navy Seals. How have you been?"

"Good, I work for the big oil companies. But thinking about handing in my notice. I often wondered how your real date went."

I laughed as I told her about my date with Gilda. We both laughed.

"We shouldn't laugh."

"What about your date?"

"He was sitting on my steps when I returned to my place. He was a nice guy. We went to dinner. It was nice."

"My dad had a heart attack that night."

"I'm sorry."

"Yeah, I moved home and never went back. Dad lived for two months after that. I told him about you. He said I should go back and see if you want to go to dinner with me. But when I did, you had already moved."

"Yeah, I was hired to inspect oil rigs on land and sea. And here I am still working for them."

"Can I take you out to dinner when we get back?"

"I would have liked nothing more, but I'm engaged to a good man. I could never hurt him."

"Well then, congratulations. When is the big day?"

"Next year, he wants to get married now, but I need to make sure it's for real. I never thought I would see you again." The guy who gave me the clothes sat down next to Gray.

"Gilly, this is my brother, Hutch."

"No wonder I thought I knew you. Your eyes are the same as my wrong date."

"Gilly, was your wrong blind date?" Hutch asked, staring at me.

"Yes, small world, right?"

"Yeah, small world."

I saw the sadness in his brother's eyes and wondered about it. I stood up. "If you two will excuse me, I need to sleep for a while."

"I'll show you the way," Grayson said, standing up.

"Thank you, Hutch has already shown me." I held onto my borrowed sweats. "Hey, these must belong to you. Thanks for the loan of them."

"You're welcome."

God, why did I feel like I wanted to cry? I wiped my hand across my face, and there were tears there. *What is the matter with me? Is it because I always thought Gray Campbell was my one true love? But that was when you were younger. You are thirty-two now, and you know better. That's how stupid I was back then. True love, what an idiot I was at twenty-four.*

He never came back to see me because his dad had a heart attack. It had nothing to do with that wild, hot kiss he gave me. *I can't think about him anymore. I've had that talk with myself before. I'm engaged to a fantastic man. I can't remember one special kiss out of all the kisses I've had from my fiancé. What is wrong with me? I never forgot the kiss Grayson Campbell gave me eight years ago. (You're thirty-two years old, Gilly; stop thinking about Grayson.)* What's crazy is I never became serious with another man because I compared all of their kisses to that one—*that one frigging kiss.* I probably imagined how it was anyway. What am I thinking I am serious about another man. I'm serious about my fiancé. I love him. *Remember that, Gillian. You are serious about Gerald.*

I went to sleep, and I dreamed about Grayson Campbell. And in my dreams, we did a lot more than kiss.

Dear reader.

Thank you, for your continued support. I really appreciate that you read my books.

If you can please leave me a review for this book, I would appreciate it enormously.

Your reviews allow me to get validation I need to keep going as an Indie author.

Just a moment of your time is all that is needed. I will try my best to give you the

best books I can write.

FOLLOW ME ON SOCIAL MEDIA
https://www.bookbub.com/profile/susie-mciver

. . .

NEWSLETTER SIGN UP HTTP://BIT.LY/SUSIEMCIVER_NEWSLETTER

FACEBOOK PAGE: www.facebook.com/SusieMcIverAuthor/

FACEBOOK GROUP: www.facebook.com/groups/SusieMcIverAuthor/

HTTPS://WWW.SUSIEMCIVER.COM/

Printed in Great Britain
by Amazon